A BODY
IN THE HOUSE

A BODY IN THE HOUSE

The Frank May Chronicles

Lawrence Friedman

A QP Mystery

QP BOOKS
New Orleans, Louisiana

A BODY IN THE HOUSE

The Frank May Chronicles

A QP Mystery, published in 2017 by QP Books.

QUID PRO, LLC
5860 Citrus Blvd., Suite D-101
New Orleans, Louisiana 70123
www.qpbooks.com

ISBN 978-1-61027-373-2 (paperback)
ISBN 978-1-61027-372-5 (eBook)

Publisher's Cataloging-in-Publication

Friedman, Lawrence.
    A body in the house / Lawrence Friedman.
      p. cm.
    Series: *The Frank May Chronicles* (#11)
    ISBN 978-1-61027-373-2 (pbk.)
1. Lawyers—California—Fiction. 2. San Mateo (Cal.)—Fiction. 3. May, Frank (Fictitious character)—Fiction. I. Friedman, Lawrence. II. Title. III. Series.
PS357.F725 2017

        813.'1'8258—dc22
        20177447634
        CIP

for Leah, Jane, Amy, Sarah,
David, Lucy, and Irene

A BODY
IN THE HOUSE

1

Margot Williams was a young woman, and a client of mine. She sat across from me in my office one bright and sunny morning telling me one of the most amazing stories I had ever heard—and believe me, I've heard some amazing stories. Lawyers, and I'm a lawyer, are used to hearing remarkable tales. It's part of the business. People expose their bodies to doctors, their souls (maybe) to clergy, and their lives—their finances, their troubles—to their lawyers.

I thought I had heard it all. But Margot's story was something completely new. Margot's problem was the dead body she found in her house. She lived with her husband, Jim, in Menlo Park, California. That's a suburb of San Francisco—south of the city, down the peninsula, part of that complex people call Silicon Valley. The area is sprinkled with brash young billionaires. None of them live in Margot's neighborhood. Her house was quite an ordinary house. It was part of a subdivision, located on a street of nearly identical houses. Outwardly identical that is; the gardens and lawns were different, and the paint jobs were different. Decent, substantial houses, but nothing special. Margot's house was painted a kind of dusky pink. The front yard was mostly lawn, with a fringe of pyracantha and rose bushes up to the property line and bordering on the sidewalk.

The life inside each house was surely different. Everybody has a story. Some of the houses on Margot's block could no doubt tell an interesting story, maybe even an exciting one. But, to the best of my knowledge, none of the neighbors had ever found corpses in their homes. Only Margot.

Some people get upset when they find a dead mouse—or even a dead spider—inside the house. Not to mention a live spider, or one of those tiny lizards that live in the shrubbery and come out in the sunshine to warm their little cold-blooded hearts. My younger daughter saw a garter snake on the driveway, and it terrified her. I can only imagine what she might do if she found a dead woman in the house.

But I have to give you a bit more background. Margot and Jim were the owners of the house. There was a mortgage, of course—doesn't everybody have a mortgage?—but it doesn't figure in this story. Margot and Jim were both young—in their late 20's—and they both had jobs. You need two incomes to live in Menlo Park. Certainly you need two incomes to buy a house, unless you inherited the property or a lot of money, or founded a company in the tech business and sold it to Google for a billion dollars. Even a simple, modest house, like the Williams' house, can be outrageously expensive.

Enough talk about real estate. Here is Margot's story. She and her husband had gone on a trip to southern California. When they returned home, late on a Sunday night, they discovered the body—to their horror. The corpse was a young woman, very dead, dead for about ten hours. They found her inside a cedar chest in the front hallway, in which they usually stored spare linen.

But I'm getting ahead of myself. I want to explain, first of all, the setting. This was, as I said, Menlo Park, in northern California. Some thirty miles south of San Francisco. Don't believe everything you hear about California. Most of us who live here are not lunatics, drug addicts, hippies, or cultists; or computer geeks, or venture capitalists, or guys who dropped out of college and who are now worth more than the Gross National Product of a mid-sized African country. Most of us are ordinary people. Of course, nobody thinks of himself or herself as ordinary. That's one of the things that makes a person ordinary. And in a way they're right. Everybody, as I said, has a story.

I have one too, but most of it is irrelevant. What's relevant is that I'm a lawyer, a member of the California bar. My name is Frank May. I am in my 40's, married (my wife's name is Celia), and I have two teenaged daughters. Celia and I have been married for 20 years. In California, that's considered an achievement.

I practice law in San Mateo County. Indeed, my office is in the City of San Mateo. I am in private practice; I have clients, but no partners. There are law firms with more than a thousand lawyers—two thousand, maybe three thousand—firms with branches all over, firms with billings in the millions and millions of dollars. Many of these gigantic firms have offices in San Francisco, in San Jose, and even in Palo Alto, the three legal capitals of Silicon Valley. The big firms also have satellite offices in New York and Washington, not to mention Hong Kong and Paris and Abu Dhabi or wherever. I don't work for one of those firms. I work for myself. I have my own small office. The partners in the big firms are rich as Croesus. But are they happy?

I suppose some of them are. Some people who drive bright yellow Tesla convertibles and own homes in six places are extremely happy, even if we wish somehow they were leading miserable lives.

But then again, some of the rest of us are happy. Without a Tesla convertible, or even a yacht.

I have a small office, in a suite with other lawyers, who, like me, are solo practitioners. We share a receptionist, who also does some paralegal work. Her name is Peggy. She is a divorced woman in her 50's, with dyed red hair. Peggy is reasonably efficient, except for her "sinus trouble," which seems to be chronic, and is a source of great misery to her, "though I don't like to complain," she says. In fact, she does like to complain. Most of us do like to complain.

The sinus problems seem to cluster around Mondays and Fridays.

The City of San Mateo, as I said, is in San Mateo County. It lies just south of San Francisco, which is at the tip of the San Francisco Bay peninsula. San Mateo (the city) is about 15 miles from the southern boundary of San Francisco. The next county to the south—it figures in this story—is Santa Clara. Many things around here are named after Spanish saints. These names are left over from the days when Mexicans, or at least the Mexican government, owned all the land. We took the land away from them, but the names linger on.

San Mateo is considered a suburb. I suppose it is a suburb and that I have a suburban practice. I don't represent Google or Facebook or Apple. My clients are mostly individuals and small businesses. Some of my clients are fine, decent hard-working people. Some of them are very definitely not. A fair percentage of them are annoying and demanding. In any event, I'm in the general practice of law. I do real estate, family law, probate matters. I represent small corporations, car wash companies, restaurants. One client manufactures small, hideous plastic novelties, or imports them from China. I don't quite know which.

I also have one or two clients who are trying to break into the big-time with what they consider killer software. I understand almost nothing about software or hardware, but the Bay Area is full of young people whose dream in life is to found a company and became a billionaire by age 30. They won't make it, of course; and if they do—or if it even seems the least bit likely—they will surely abandon me and go with a big and expensive firm, either in Palo Alto or San Francisco. Meanwhile, pending the billions, they're mine.

Above all, I handle wills, trusts, and estate planning. Some of my best clients turn out to be dead. I prefer it when they die a natural death. Amazingly, this doesn't always happen.

Lawyers, suburban or not, can go through a lifetime of practice, handle thousands of matters, deal with hundreds of clients—and never have anything to do with an unnatural death. Certainly never with murder. That is, unless they are criminal lawyers, which I most certainly am not. That's a specialty of its own. The rest of us never touch the stuff.

Personally, I am the furthest thing from a man of violence. I lead a quiet life. Well, mostly quiet. My wife, Celia, teaches English literature in a local high school. Except for the fact that we don't have a dog (Celia is allergic), we qualify as fairly typical. The other people on our block are mostly thirty- and forty-year-olds, solidly middleclass: accountants, engineers, a pediatrician, a dentist or two. The houses are well kept, the paint is fresh. Roses grow in front. No doubt each house—like the houses on Margot's block—harbors its own little secrets, its own skeletons in the closet. Rumor has it that the couple in the house five doors down, a house that's painted a kind of obscene green, are "swingers," whatever that means. I barely know them. Maybe the green paint stimulates an offbeat sex life.

To the best of my knowledge, whatever sins and transgressions—and there are many—form the suburban repertoire, murder is not one of them.

And yet my client, Margot Williams, found a dead body in her house. I listened to her story, and I couldn't help thinking: what kind of fate or karma or nemesis pursues me? Why do so many of my clients get themselves killed or wind up in the middle of a real-life Agatha Christie or Sue Grafton novel?

It was January—late January—as I think I said. The rainy season. Our wintertime, such as it is. Some people say California is boring, weather-wise, because it doesn't have seasons. We do have seasons. There are two seasons: Perfect and Less than Perfect. Perfect is summer, and parts of spring and fall. Summer is without humidity or mosquitoes. The days are warm, but not too warm, and the nights cool, ideal for sleeping. The winter months are the Less than Perfect Season, because they can be chilly, even frosty at times, and because (except in drought years), you can expect it to rain. In the Perfect Season, it never rains. In the Less than Perfect season, it sometimes rains. I remember the day I spoke to Margot. It was dull, overcast. The clouds seemed pregnant with the possibility of rain. Margot Williams was more agitated than I had ever seen her. And no wonder.

A few years shy of thirty, Margot was and is good-looking, medium height, with soft brown hair and brown eyes. I can't say I knew her well; but she always struck me as nice, whatever that means. Decent, polite, well-spoken. Someone who would never knowingly inflict pain or suffering on other people.

Sweet. Honest. I would never have expected her to be connected, however distantly, with a mysterious and cold-blooded murder.

Williams was her married name. She was old fashioned enough to be married in the first place, and to take her husband's name, in the second place. Her husband Jim (James Arthur Williams, to be precise) was working for Stanford University at the time. I was never sure exactly what he did—I think he worked in the planning office, or the business office, or the fund-raising office. Something to do with money. Money is the lifeblood of any large institution, public or private. He had a degree in accounting. Jim's business was money.

Margot worked at Stanford, too, but in another department—she was some sort of low-level administrator. The University is, in a way, a big business. I read somewhere that the endowment is about 19 billion dollars. That's a huge amount of money. Stanford has a budget in the hundreds of millions and it's one of the biggest employers in northern California. Maybe the biggest. The Harvard of the West. Thousands of people work for Stanford. Walmart has more employees, of course; but how many Nobel Prize winners are on the payroll of Walmart?

I met Margot a few years before all this happened, before she was married. Her name was Margot Davis. Margot was an only child. Her parents had been well-to-do people; they married late. Her father was part owner of a chain of carwashes. He was a frugal investor, and bought real estate at just the right time. He died when Margot was in high school. Margot went to college in Santa Cruz. A few years later, her mother died in an automobile accident.

Margot's mother had been a good friend of one of our neighbors; and they had been friendly with Margot as well. When her mother died, Margot needed a lawyer to handle the estate. The neighbor recommended me. I was glad to get the business. Margot's mother had been careful with her money, and had planned well; she had a will, which a local lawyer had drawn up for her. Fortunately for me, the lawyer was no longer in business; he had retired and moved to a development for senior citizens in Las Vegas. Why anybody would want to do that is a mystery to me. I don't mean retirement, that I can understand, I mean living in Las Vegas. I suppose if you're born there, you have no choice. But to move there voluntarily? The world is full of people, I suppose, who make strange decisions. There are people, after all, who move to Alaska of their own free will.

Anyway, Margot needed a lawyer, and I was only too happy to step into the picture. Mrs. Davis left her estate, naturally, to her only child. It was a simple estate to handle. I almost felt guilty collecting the fee. Almost, but not quite.

For a brief period, Margot lived in Los Angeles. That's where she met Jim, fell in love, and got married. I was invited to the wedding, but I didn't go. It was in Los Angeles, and I didn't feel like making the trip. I don't like weddings. Especially big weddings. The ceremony itself is painless. Everybody goes ooh and ah when they see the bride appear in her beautiful gown and the bridesmaids also look wonderful in their matching dresses. The party afterwards is what I find totally repulsive. The groom's buddies—headed by the best man—get drunk and tell coarse, unfunny stories about their friend. Then comes the deafening music of the dance band.

Sometimes the food is good.

Actually, Margot's wedding was quite small. Nevertheless, I didn't go. We gave them a gift, of course. She was a client, after all. Celia is in charge of wedding presents. I'm a liberated male, and I consider myself a staunch feminist for the most part. But there are limits. For me, anyway. I don't do laundry (maybe I should). Picking out wedding gifts is another thing I avoid. Margot and Jim were registered at some department store, and I think we gave them silverware, in the hideous pattern they had picked out for themselves. After that, Margot was off my radar. Like most people, she had no particular need to consult me. In general, the less you have to do with lawyers, the better.

I did hear—from one of our neighbors—that she and Jim had moved to the Bay Area and bought a house in Sharon Heights, a few miles from the Stanford campus. That, I thought to myself, must have eaten up her entire inheritance. Or close to it. Unless you bought your house twenty years ago (as I did), nothing within miles of the campus sells for less than a million dollars. If you sell your house in Buffalo, New York, or Des Moines, Iowa—that is, your big, beautiful house on an acre lot, with four bedrooms, three baths, and a whole forest of shade trees—the proceeds might buy you a mobile home in Palo Alto. If you could find one. Basically, affordable houses don't exist.

Little did I think that I would ever see them again, or at least not for years. It was a shock when she appeared in my office, after a rather frantic phone call, and sat there, telling me a story that seemed almost too bizarre to believe.

*　*　*

At any rate, here is Margot's story. It was January, as I said, and apparently things were quiet at work, for both of them. I guess the money business is slow at Stanford, in January. They probably work overtime in December, trying to induce rich alumni to give money before the year ends. Margot and Jim had decided to take a mini-vacation. They drove south, down Highway 101, a beautiful drive. They spent a day or two in the desert, in Palm Springs, where it was warm and sunny, then a couple of days in Los Angeles. Then they started back north, along Highway 1, the spectacular winding road along the coast, taking in the sights, including Hearst Castle at San Simeon, that fantastic monument to a man with great wealth and an ego as monumental as the castle. The weather can be tricky along the coast in January, but they had good luck. No rain at all, and very little fog.

They spent the last two nights in Carmel. Carmel is a small coastal town, all little boutique hotels and boutique boutiques, much beloved of tourists. Clint Eastwood was the mayor at one time. God knows why. Anyway, Margot said, the trip had been like a second honeymoon—and she particularly enjoyed Carmel. Again, the weather was unusually good. They stayed at a small motel, a few blocks from Ocean Avenue, a simple, pleasant place, built in imitation colonial style. More like a cluster of cottages than a motel, not one of those polyester palaces.

They spent Saturday sight-seeing, they had a good dinner in Carmel, sea-food and wine, walked around the streets looking at the tourists, strolled on the beach in the moonlight, then went to bed. All very romantic. In the morning, Margot slept late, then stayed in bed for a while, pampering herself and reading the morning newspaper. Jim went jogging. He came back; they showered, ate brunch slowly and lazily at a local restaurant, and got ready to go.

She had, she said, that kind of nice, soft vacation feeling, where you wish the vacation could just go on. She hated to give up and go back to her humdrum life. "It was such a nice vacation," she said. In retrospect, this seems ironic. The sun was shining in Carmel; it was more like May than January. But they were both due at work on Monday, so they had to get back. Still, they took their time going home. Normally, the trip from Carmel to their house should take about two hours, or less, but they were in no particular rush.

They took the coast road again. They made a detour at Castroville, a dinky little town that calls itself the "artichoke capital of the world." The town is very proud of this rather odd distinction. Why not? Gilroy, which is close to San Jose, calls itself the "garlic capital of the world." Why artichokes and garlic need capitals is difficult to say. Between the two, I would choose to be the artichoke capital. Garlic is all right in its place, of course, but it's a limited place.

Margot wanted to stop in Castroville, and they did. They bought fried artichoke hearts and munched on them. Then they drove to Santa Cruz and parked in the downtown area. Margot wanted to look at antique stores. The fog came in unexpectedly. I know that kind of fog from experience; it covers the whole scene with a pale, gray, pearly light. A velvet haze envelops the old Victorian houses and the tops of the roller coasters, and the boardwalk has a dreamlike appearance. The air gets damp to the touch, but it's a beautiful sort of damp.

Margot told me that she likes to poke around in antique stores. In one small, dirty store, she found an ancient wicker chair, broken and battered, but it spoke to her. The chair was in terrible shape, but she really wanted it—wanted to buy it on the spot. Jim turned stubborn. He asked her where they would put it, since the house was cluttered up already. "Husbands are like that," she said. "Of course, in the end, they usually give way." But this time, Jim seemed insistent, so she decided to humor him. She simply wrote down the information (price, name of store, and so on), and they left and went back to the car.

"I suppose you're wondering why I'm telling you all these things, these little details," she said. "I want you to know why we took so long to get back. The police wanted to know everything about our trip. Where we were, and when. What time this happened, what time that happened, why did you stop, and so on. Are you sure you were gone so long, can you prove it, why did you make these stops, and can you prove it? Anyway, we can. Not the fried artichokes, but the antique store. They'll remember us, I said, they even know our names."

At any rate, on that Sunday, it was late afternoon by the time they crossed the mountains on Highway 17, a fast and treacherous road that links Santa Cruz to San Jose. It was already dark when they reached San Jose. She told Jim she was hungry—the only lunch they had had were those artichoke hearts. So they stopped at a fast food place and bought hamburgers, French fries, and milk shakes. Then—only then—did they drive up the peninsula, and head for home. It was much later than they had expected.

In fact, it was nearly eight o'clock in the evening when they reached the house. They lived in a part of Menlo Park called Sharon Heights. Their street was called San Benito Lane. They were tired, of course; it had been a long drive. The house was pitch-dark, and silent.

Margot had left a key with a boy who lived nearby. His name was Teddy Gilchrist. He was sixteen or seventeen years old, and very reliable. A lively kid, mature for his age, friendly, talkative and responsible. Teddy was supposed to water the plants every other day, take in the mail and the newspapers, and leave them on the sofa in the living room. At night he was instructed to turn on an outdoor light, and a light in the kitchen and the living room—a time-honored trick to fool particularly dim-witted burglars.

Teddy had no instructions about what to do on Sunday night. There was, of course, no mail. Margot couldn't remember the exact schedule for watering the plants. Maybe he was supposed to water them on Sunday. But that would be in the morning. Margot had told him they would be back by early afternoon, long before dark. As it was, they arrived much later. Teddy, of course, had not turned on the lights. The house was wrapped in total darkness. It was a cloudy and moonless night.

Margot described the house to me. It was, she said, nothing special. It was a two-story house, more or less in what you might call colonial style. It was painted a kind of dusty pink, as I think I mentioned. Shingle roof. There were three bedrooms upstairs, a couple of bathrooms and a tiny sewing room or study. Downstairs, there was a small entrance hall. As you came in the front door, the stairs were directly in front of you. The kitchen and dining room were off to the left side; on the right side there was the living room. Tucked away under the stairs was a half-bath. They also had a two-car garage. The garage was at the side of the house—to the left, as you faced the front of the house from the street. There was a gravel driveway, and the garage had a door leading into the kitchen, at one side. The garage was filled with suitcases, boxes, ten-speed bicycles, miscellaneous junk, and garden tools. Everything but cars. That, I must say, is typical of California. Nobody would dream of actually putting a car into the garage. Normally, there's no room for the car. Anyway, why would you need to park a car inside? It's not as if it needs protection from the elements. In California, the elements are on vacation.

It was their habit, Margot said, to park the car in the driveway just in front of the garage. They would enter the house through the kitchen, using the door that opened into the house from the garage. This door was locked, just as the front door was. Teddy, as far as they knew, had the only other key.

Most of the houses on the block, she told me, were more or less similar, indeed, pretty much identical in shape and design, because they were built by the same developer about ten years earlier. I can confirm this—after I talked to Margot, out of sheer curiosity, I drove down her street. The houses were painted different colors, but I suppose that's less obvious in the dark, or not obvious at all. And of course there were variations in landscaping: some people went in for groundcover (ivy, or ice-plant); some people for rose bushes, or juniper; one or two had rocks and gravel, Japanese style. The Williams house had mostly lawn in front, with a fringe of pyracantha bushes.

Sharon Heights is a few miles from the Stanford campus. It's a quiet, residential area, near a small shopping center, with grocery stores, bakeries, and miscellaneous shops. Sharon Heights is a nice place to live, if you like that sort of place. Very quiet. Not the place for the young and restless, I would imagine; but a good place to raise a family.

I couldn't resist asking Margot the obvious question: "Could somebody have made a mistake about the house? I mean, could somebody have confused it with another house on the same block? I don't want to insult your house; but you said the houses around there are, well, pretty much alike."

"I guess our house isn't very different, to be perfectly honest," she said. "Especially in the dark."

This had occurred to me. In the dark, someone made a mistake, and left the body in the wrong house. Did that mean the neighbors were the main suspects? But then again, how did they get in? You had to wonder about that.

Margot went on with her story: Jim backed the car into the space in front of the garage door. She was the one who opened the inner door—that is, the door to the kitchen; she took the key out of her purse, unlocked the door, and switched on the kitchen light.

Everything, as far as she could see, was completely in order. Nothing struck her as strange, or out of place. The house was quiet, drowsy. She noted the plants in the kitchen, and later upstairs. Well watered, she thought, Teddy did his job, as she knew he would. Meanwhile, Jim brought in the suitcases. He took them upstairs and put them on the bed. She came upstairs, opened one of the suitcases, and took out a little dish, something she bought in Carmel. She began to unpack her suitcase.

Jim had gone back, locked the car, and was now using the upstairs bathroom. That gave Margot a chance to sneak downstairs. Before leaving on their trip, she had bought Jim a gift. Monday was Jim's half-birthday; he was twenty-eight and a half years old. Half-birthdays don't mean much to most people, but it was a special thing between her and Jim. They had met on one of Jim's half-birthdays. The present was a book about tennis. Jim had a passion for tennis. She bought the book at a bookstore in Palo Alto. She had it gift-wrapped, then hid it away in a chest that stood in the front hallway, against the side of the staircase—an old-fashioned, wooden chest, which once belonged to her grandmother. Margot kept a few linens inside, and the chest was never locked. Mostly it was there for decoration. Eagerly, she opened the chest, looking forward to giving Jim a wonderful surprise.

That's when it happened. That's when *she* got a surprise—when she saw the dead body in the chest. A woman's body. Margot stood there in shock, then screamed and screamed and screamed.

"I knew she was dead, as soon as I saw her, the way the body was all crumpled up. She had a horrible kind of stare ... and her hands ... they looked like they were clutching something. Oh God, it was awful. I've never seen anything so awful in my life."

It must have been quite a scene. I pictured them coming in, tired, with that sense of relief you have after a trip: home at last. Maybe they planned on going to bed early, or watching a little TV in bed, maybe they thought, "we'll finish unpacking in the morning." Maybe they were thinking of making love—in their own bedroom this time—or maybe they had nothing much on their minds at all. And then this nightmare, this awful thing, this dead body invading their home. "A woman," Margot said. "It was ghastly."

"And—I have to ask—you didn't recognize this person?"

"A total stranger," she said, "I think. I mean, I'm sure. Not that I got much of a look. I ... I just stood there and screamed.

Jim came running downstairs. He stood and stared at that thing ... he was as white as a sheet. We were both ... sort of paralyzed. I couldn't move, I absolutely couldn't move," she said. "Jim kept saying 'My God' over and over. I finally stopped screaming and I said, 'Jim who is that?' He said, 'Jesus, I don't know.' I said, 'I opened this chest, this trunk, and there she was ...' I was trembling like a leaf. I think Jim was ... like me ... but he didn't scream ... after a minute or two, he calmed me down, we got a grip on ourselves. Jim asked, 'Good God, why did you open the chest?' I told him about the present, the present for his half-birthday and I said, 'Jim, what is this? This is horrible! What'll we do?'"

I don't remember the rest very clearly. Jim, well, he was calmer than I was, I couldn't even move; Jim is better than I am, I think, in a crisis. He called the police, he called an ambulance ... pretty soon the whole place was full of people."

She went on. "The ambulance came first. But she was dead. We both knew it ... we didn't touch the body or anything. Frank, I just wasn't functioning. It was a total nightmare. Jim had to take care of everything. I just folded. And the police asked so many questions. And took pictures. Later there were people from the newspapers, TV. God, it was horrible."

"You poor thing," I said.

"You know, I was so terribly ashamed of myself the next day. For going totally to pieces. That night, I couldn't sleep a wink, I kept tossing and turning. I think I fell asleep around five in the morning. When I woke up, I felt like a total fool. And the worst thing is, it's not over. It goes on and on. The whole thing must be a terrible mistake. I don't know who that woman is, I mean was, or why she was killed—why somebody dumped her in our house, or how they got in, or anything. I feel so...vulnerable. People keep asking me questions, invading my privacy, Jim's privacy. Jim is so upset—maybe even more than I am—but you know, guys, they don't feel like they can show it. He took two days off of work, I mean, I couldn't do that, so I went to the office, but I just sat there staring into space. Meanwhile, the whole street is still crawling with photographers. It's been a week, and they don't go away."

"And you're sure you didn't recognize her, Margot? You have no idea who she was?"

"No, Frank, no idea, nothing. It was horrible to look at her. But yes, she was a stranger. To Jim, too. We never laid eyes on her before. Oh God, she looked so ... dead."

"What did the police say? Have they identified her?"

"I told you, Jim called them. I was half-conscious, I swear. The most awful moment of my life. The police were all over the place. But what could we tell them? Nothing. Just our story— how we had been away—and all that. Not that they thought we had killed her or something. We found out she had been dead for hours and hours. Since about noon, maybe—and we were a hundred miles away."

"And ... they've identified her?"

"I don't think so. Listen, Frank, you've got to help us."

I said, "Of course, I'll help you—if I can. But I'm a lawyer. I don't see the connection. I mean, nobody's accusing you of anything, or Jim ... am I right?"

"I think they believe us when we say we don't know this woman, who she is, or how she got there. And when she died we were on the road, or just leaving Carmel, or whatever. Oh God, it's so creepy. We were driving north, happy as clams after a wonderful vacation, and, meanwhile, here somebody was ... doing this terrible thing. Killing this woman and dumping her in our house. Our house! God knows why. Oh, Frank, like I said, we need your help, we need it badly. I'm at my wit's end. We need advice, and somebody to act as our spokesman, somebody to tell us what to do, how to behave, what to tell the newspapers. I trust you, Frank."

"Really ..."

"And there's something else. They say you have ... a knack."

"A knack? Meaning what, Margot?"

"They say you, well, you've helped out in other cases. Situations like mine. There was this woman I know, she's in my book club ..."

"Oh God, Margot, really. Listen to me. Don't believe everything you hear."

"Please, Frank," she said. "I know you're a modest guy. But I've heard things. This friend of mine, Doris Mobius, lovely woman, she told me you were wonderful at, well, things like this."

I knew what was coming, and I remembered Doris very well.

"I mean," Margot said, "from what she told me—and I heard it from other people too—there was this incident with Doris, and the police were completely baffled, and you, well, you helped out and actually solved the case. And, she said, you're modest, you don't like to brag, but you had done that sort of thing before, she said you have a kind of gift ..."

There it was again. No matter how I tried, those rumors persisted. Frank May, 'the great detective.' Of course, there was nothing to it at all. Dumb luck, once or twice. "Margot, you know that's not the issue ... I'll do what I can. But don't expect miracles."

"But I do," she said.

I sighed. There had been a few incidents before, in which, somehow, I played a role and helped unravel a mystery or two, including some that completely baffled the police. But I'm not blaming the police. Sometimes, you have to know people. It's all very well to look for fingerprints and hair fibers or whatever, but that doesn't necessarily tell you what you want to know.

Anyway, Margot seemed to know about these incidents from Doris. And Margot was desperate, caught up in a nightmare. The only way out, as far as she could see, was to solve the mystery: identify the victim, find the killer, and put the nightmare away. She saw me as her chance, and considered me not a lawyer, but a detective.

And in one recent instance, yes, I did play a role. Actually, my success was due to an insight Celia had. She has more sense than I do; at least she's better at reading character. But she is also adamant at warning me to mind my own business and stay out of these sordid affairs. "You're a lawyer, my dear," she says, "stick to your job."

But here I was, facing Margot, and she really felt I could help her. I tried to talk to her, to play down my reputation. I think I succeeded, at least in part. I think she realized I was not exactly a skilled detective, or even an amateur detective—but she still felt I could help her, and I said I would. It was the least I could do. I promised to "keep my eyes and ears open," and do what I could, thinking, of course, that "what I could" would amount to absolutely zero.

I kept hoping the police would solve the bloody case. It was their business. Or the detectives. Whatever it is they do. But the case stayed unsolved, and got more and more tangled. If I could have peered ahead, into my crystal ball, I would have run away as fast as my legs could carry me. Another person was going to die an unnatural death. But that came later.

Meanwhile, a horn honked outside. "It's Jim," Margot explained. I walked her downstairs. She said, "The first night, neither of us slept, I think. Well, maybe Jim did, a little. He's much calmer than I am. In the morning, we could barely drag ourselves out of bed … Jim had such a headache! As I said before, he didn't want to go to work. I felt I had to go. Plus, I was miserable—and scared—and I needed company. My coworkers were really fantastic."

Jim was standing by the car, stretching his long legs, and looking at his watch. The car was a Toyota, dark red, a nice car. The morning fog had long since lifted, and a feeble sun poked above the horizon. The air was hazy, chill, and weak. There was a kind of desperation in the sky.

I smiled and shook hands with Jim. He was slender, lanky, with dark blonde hair and grey eyes. He spoke very little, and he seemed, well, on edge, like a coiled spring. I suppose this affair was as upsetting to him as it was to Margot. "But he can't show it," she told me. "Some men are like that. They think they can't have emotions. I cry and cry about this, and he just sits there brooding. It's like nothing happened. He won't let on to anybody how awful he feels. I'm trying to get him to open up, but it's hard for him."

I understood perfectly. I hear the same sort of complaint from Celia. I keep things bottled up too. We haven't found a dead body in our house, so there's no scientific test of what my reaction might be. Which is just as well.

Jim was a good-looking man. He looked very California—I can't quite explain this. Maybe he was dealing with the incident in his own way. Maybe he was used to emotional trauma; and it helped him in this crisis. His life, I learned, had not been exactly smooth. Margot told me about him. He was an only child. His father died when he was very little; his mother was pushy and neurotic. She drank heavily, and paid little attention to him. Margot was an only child, too. They bonded when they met because they both felt somewhat alone.

Now they were partners in misery.

* * *

Jim and Margot drove off together, and I walked back to my office. I stared at my building. Somehow the stucco had never looked so cheap. There was a courtyard in the middle of the building; a small, miserable fountain trickled sadly, surrounded by agave plants. The leaves were turning brown. The plants looked stiff and unhealthy. They sat there helplessly while the bugs chewed away at their ribs. Why does the landlord grow those things? I felt depressed. Winter depresses me, even California winter, or maybe especially. I think it's the dampness, the sickly sunshine, and the hazy, unhealthy air.

And suddenly, too, the circumstances came flooding back into my mind. No wonder Margot woke up crying; no wonder Jim's head throbbed. It was a nightmare, a total, absolute nightmare. I thought of that woman, young and dead, blonde, pretty, stuffed in a chest, robbed of every stitch of identity, strangled by someone—robbed of her life. Who would do such a thing ... and why?

And who *was* she, after all?

2

At any rate, this awful thing happened on a Sunday, in January. After my meeting with Margot, I looked for the story in one of the local papers. I live in San Mateo County and I get the *San Francisco Chronicle* at home. Apparently, nobody reads newspapers any more, well, nobody under 30. I guess people do read—or at least look at—local papers, which land in your mailbox, and are free. I make it my business to look at our local paper, and some of the papers of surrounding towns. At least I glance at them. I try to keep abreast of local events as well as real estate, zoning matters, that sort of thing. I don't usually pay much attention to crime news—such as it is—or stories about who won some high school football game, or what was playing at the multiplex. As far as problems with sewer lines, traffic, and new parking rules for major streets, I put them in the same category as the war in Syria and international arms control. Vitally important, but excessively boring. I also avoid reading all the tips about gardening, which appear with deadly regularity. I like gardens—doesn't everybody? But I have no interest in reading about mulch, or whether this flower or that is best planted in the shade. Gardening bores me. All this stuff about mulch and composts and the cures for whitefly: no thank you.

I guessed I had missed the story about the body in the cedar chest. I found it in a week-old paper, which, happily, we had neither thrown out nor consigned to the recycle bin. The headline read: "Dead Body Found in Local Home." The Williams name was, mercifully, not mentioned. I was glad that the paper seemed anxious to protect their privacy.

According to the story, the body had not been identified. Nobody had stepped forward to claim it. No report of a missing person matched the deceased. The corpse was a woman with dark blonde hair and bluish-green eyes, in her late 20's. She had been strangled. There was no purse, no money, no credit cards or papers: nothing to indicate who she was. There was no evidence of "recent sexual activity or rape," as the story put it. She was, however, pregnant—second or third month, according to the newspaper. Her clothes were in order—slacks, a blouse, underwear—everything of good quality, but nothing unusual, and nothing that could be easily traced.

I looked at the newspaper files in the local branch library. I found nothing further about the case. The papers were full of stories about sexual harassment. Apparently, there was this policeman in San Carlos, who liked to fondle the breasts of women drivers. He watched, with an eagle eye, for minor traffic infractions such as illegal U-turns, and if the woman was attractive, and alone in the car, he was instantly on the case. This seemed pretty sick to me, and the women, quite naturally, were indignant or traumatized or horrified. There was one woman, though, who refused to give her name, and who said, "he ended up not giving me a ticket, so I felt, well, a deal is a deal." There was also news about a high school teacher in Atherton, a married woman of 35, who "seduced" (that was the word in the story) two boys from her American history class.

But surely, I thought, the mystery is going to be solved. There'll be fingerprints or other kinds of evidence. A witness to the crime. Somebody who saw somebody bring the body into the house. Or something. They'll make an arrest. Everything will go back to normal.

How wrong I was.

3

The next day, as it happened, I had lunch with a fellow lawyer, Sylvan Platt, who practices law in Palo Alto. He is a member of a three-lawyer firm, with an office on University Avenue. They call these small, specialized firms "boutique firms." Sylvan and his partners specialize in estate planning and work of that type. From time to time, we had clients who had dealings with each other. It was Sylvan who asked me to lunch. "Long time no see, Frank," he said, "let's do lunch. Tuesday?" Tuesday was fine. "Can we meet in Palo Alto," he asked. "I have to see one of my clients there, a psychology professor, Stanford professor, big pain in the ass, and I'm a little squeezed for time." I said sure.

At the time, his casual remark meant nothing to me, except that I would have to drive ten miles from my office to meet him and have lunch. But I'm an agreeable guy, and when Sylvan, a real foodie, mentioned a Chinese restaurant that I liked a lot, I certainly had no objection. I looked forward to the meal.

Traffic was horrendous, and I got to the restaurant later than I expected. Sylvan was already there. He was a man in his 50's, big and jovial, with a protruding chin which reminded me a bit of old pictures of Mussolini, though nobody could be less like an Italian dictator than Sylvan. He was somewhat overweight and he had a booming voice, which he lowered, of course, whenever he talked business. He was immaculately dressed in a navy blue suit, white shirt, and a quiet necktie with geometric designs. He did have rings on most of his fingers, and a gold wristwatch that I would guess was quite expensive.

He had a tendency to dominate conversations. It wasn't just the voice; it was his manner in general. Nobody could accuse Sylvan Blatt of introversion. But he was not a bad guy at all. He was wickedly intelligent, larger than life—a bit brash and over the top. I liked him. So did most people, I imagine.

After a bit of small talk, about the weather, I asked, "How's Tessa?" I was pleased with myself, for actually remembering her name. I think I met her once.

Sylvan looked at me. "Oh, Frank, I guess you didn't know. We're divorced. Do you know, she turned anorexic; can you believe it, at her age? Ate nothing but green peppers and fat-free cottage cheese. You should have seen our refrigerator! Oh, she drank beer—and diet root beer. She got to be all skin and bones, she was horrendously depressed, I mean, she was a mess; wouldn't see a therapist, you can imagine what our sex life was like. Or wasn't like. I couldn't take it after a while. Imagine, green peppers. I never want to see one again. So we split."

"Sorry, Sylvan."

"Don't be sorry. Best thing that ever happened to me. And to Tessa, as it turned out. She's into yoga now, and she's quit dieting, she's eating tons of carbohydrates, rice, pasta, mashed potatoes, and every species of bread on earth. Hot fudge sundaes. Gained tons of weight; and she's dating, I think. She goes on the web, that's what everybody does. She found a site for recovering anorexics, they're mostly women, but there were some guys. A folk singer, would you believe it? Anyway, that's water under the bridge. I'm a lonely bachelor now."

I said something innocuous. Sylvan said: "Hey, Frank, I'm not sensitive on the subject. And don't believe me when I say lonely. But if you think I'm going to tell you about my sexual exploits, you have another think coming."

"I wouldn't dream of asking," I said.

"I hear from the grapevine," Sylvan said, "that you're up to your ears in this latest murder thing, the body in the house in Sharon Heights."

"The owner of the house is my client," I said. "But 'up to my ears,' no, that's not right."

"Hey, Frank, we all know what a modest guy you are. Listen: I want to know everything. All the details. Maybe if you tell me, I'll have a bright idea. Maybe I can help you solve the case."

"I thought you were squeezed for time."

"I was, as far as getting here was concerned. I had to talk to this client of mine, he's got real marital problems. Psychology professor. Ramsey Hardcastle. Right now, I've got all the time in the world. I have nothing on this afternoon. There's stuff I could do, but what the hell."

I paid no attention to the name he mentioned. Not at the time. Professor Ramsey Hardcastle. Later on it would become extremely meaningful.

I let Sylvan do the ordering, which he did with great gusto. Meanwhile, I told him the story, in full detail.

"Margot and Jim both swear," I said, "that they don't have the foggiest notion who she might be. I suppose they could be lying. Still ... now here's the strangest thing: we know roughly *when* this woman died. The Williamses came home in the evening, some time between seven and eight o'clock—anyway, I think so. At that time, this woman had been dead quite a while. Somewhere between six or eight or ten hours. The police aren't sure exactly. About seven or eight hours, maybe nine or ten, that's their best guess. Maybe a little longer."

"So what does that mean?"

"So she died, let's say, noon on Sunday, or late morning. Something like that."

"But that's crazy," Sylvan said. The food had come. Sylvan had done the ordering for both of us. That was, of course, the right thing to do. The food was delicious.

"Food is great here," he said. "This restaurant should be in Zagat's. Frank, are you on for dessert? I'm going to get mango pudding. Fabulous, and not really fattening. Not that I care, these days ... I'm pampering myself."

I suspect that Sylvan made a habit of pampering himself. When the mango pudding arrived—I had stuck to my guns and declined dessert—Sylvan ate half of it with great relish, then paused, waved his spoon around and said: "I'm trying to eat more slowly though. People say you enjoy it more. And you should pause to catch your breath. This pudding is delicious, by the way." Then he said, "Let me get this straight. Somebody killed this woman, late morning, or maybe around noon, on a Sunday morning. Maybe she didn't die right away, but anyway. Then this guy, this killer—I'm going to guess it's a guy—he drags the body of this dying woman, or maybe she's already dead, into a house in Sharon Heights, although there's no sign of a break-in. The house happens to be empty, because the people are away. They're on the highway, driving up from Carmel, to be exact, at that moment. Wherever. They're on the road, though, somewhere miles away. Then this killer stuffs the body into a chest. All this, of course, in broad daylight."

"Isn't there another possibility?" I said. "I mean, the broad daylight part, that's not necessarily true. Suppose she was killed *inside* the house. Somebody made an arrangement to meet her there. They had a fight, and the guy killed her. Of course, under those circumstances, nobody would see it, and there's no need to assume he dragged the body in from outside. It would have to be somebody who knew that the people weren't home, right? Mind you, a person could drive a car up the driveway, and there's a way in through the kitchen. Anyway, that's what Margot told me—you could sneak a body in that way, maybe wrapped up in something. Nobody would see you."

"That part sounds weird. So does the other part," Sylvan said. "This guy, he agrees to meet this woman, in an empty house. What for? They're having some sort of tryst, maybe? Making love in an empty house?"

He finished off the pudding, smacking his lips. "Hey, Frank," he said. "Maybe this is it. They're a weird couple. They get a sexual charge from having sex in an empty house. They break into houses, that's part of the thrill. Like, they're burglars and sex fiends. But something goes wrong, and bang! She's dead."

"Good try, Sylvan," I said. "But she wasn't raped or anything."

"I didn't say rape. I said sex. Never mind."

"Anyway," I said, "How did the killer get in? For what it's worth, Margot says, there's no sign of a fight, no blood, nothing disturbed. The house was just the way they left it. They went over it, checked everything. How did this couple—the weirdos—how did they get in?"

"Easy," Sylvan said. "Burglars know how to do it. And the killer had hours and hours to clean up his act, if he needed the time. So that proves nothing. Hey, Frank, did you say something about a key?"

"They left a key with a kid in the neighborhood. He came by, watered the plants, and took in the mail. He maybe stopped by Sunday morning, according to Margot. Everything in order. He noticed nothing at all. No one on the block saw anything, heard anything, nothing. I got all this from Margot. No witnesses at all. But it's a quiet neighborhood, and people tend to come and go in their cars. Margot says the police checked everybody on the block. No information. At least that's what they told Margot."

"And her story, Margot's story, checks out?"

"They were in Carmel. The people at the motel remember them. They didn't leave until late morning. They had brunch, came back to their room, and paid the bill, then left, oh, around 12:45. It would have been impossible for them to drive here, murder the woman, and drive back. Oh yes, they stopped various places; and I guess those things check out too. They're telling the truth."

"And the kid, the one with the key? Did he lose it, or misplace it?"

"I don't know. Margot says he's a good kid, careful, conscientious. They've used him before. He likes to earn money, they pay him, and he's reliable. That's what they say."

"What about his folks?"

"No dad. Just a mother. Maybe she got hold of the key, but why would she do this? She's a suburban housewife. A school teacher. I don't know anything about the father; he's dead or someplace else. Kid is an only child."

"Well, somebody broke in, that has to be it," Sylvan said. "These houses aren't hard to get into, for a professional, I think. Did they have a burglar alarm? Some people do."

"I have no idea."

"Then you should find out, my friend," Sylvan said.

"Find out? Why, Sylvan? I have nothing to do with this. I'm not finding out anything. As Samuel Goldwyn said, 'include me out.'"

"Oh, Frank, you're a real card. Come on, you don't fool me."

I realized there was no point in arguing. Meanwhile, we had just gotten the bill and two fortune cookies. If I was expecting wisdom and guidance, I was doomed to disappointment; in fact, my fortune was a blank. Was this an omen?

As we left the restaurant, Sylvan seemed in a very good humor. He had enjoyed the lunch. My stock had gone up. I was the lawyer for Margot Williams—this made me close to the heart of an intriguing mystery—and Sylvan (as he told me) loved mysteries.

"It's the way I relax," he said. "Now that Tessa is gone, I read two or three every week. And here's a real life mystery, right in our backyard, sort of. That's great. Maybe you'll solve it. Hey, listen," he continued, "I've got a theory for you. This kid who waters the plants, he's the one that killed her. He's actually not a kid at all, but a midget; and he kills for the fun of it." Sylvan meant this as a joke, and he found it extremely funny. He laughed all the way to the car. I was, to put it mildly, not amused.

His car was a black Mercedes. "Isn't she a beauty?" he said. "Cost a fortune, though. But what the hell. I'm a divorced guy now. I have to impress the chicks, don't I?" He laughed again.

He got into the car and lowered the window. "Frank, I know you're onto this thing. This murder thing. Here's my advice. Find out who she was. The dead woman. That's the key to everything. When you know who she was, you'll know why somebody killed her, and who. So that's where you start. Who was she?"

"Sylvan," I said, "I wouldn't know where to start. Whatever you might think, I'm not a detective, not even as a hobby. There's no way I could find out who this woman was."

But I was wrong. I would in fact do exactly that: find out who she was. And it happened quite soon.

4

The very next day, when I got to my office, rather later than usual, I saw a teenaged boy waiting in the hallway outside the office door. That was unusual enough. Clients come to see me all the time, but by appointment. Once in a great while, there's a walk-in, but it's never a teenager. I know a little bit about the habits of the young—I have two adolescent daughters, after all—and trotting off to see a lawyer is not one of those habits. But this was not your typical teenager, as I would soon find out.

"Mr. May?"

"Yes?"

He reached out his hand, and said, "I'm Teddy Gilchrist." It took me a minute or two to remember who this was. Margot's neighbor. The kid with the key.

He was about seventeen, I would guess, a high school student no doubt. He was scrawny, with a slightly receding chin, very dark, intelligent eyes. At least they looked intelligent. There were traces of acne on his face. He was wearing the uniform of his cohort: blue jeans, a t-shirt, and flip-flops. His jeans were torn at the knee, and badly faded, but of course, as I know from my daughters and the boys they occasionally drag into the house, that was, if anything, the height of fashion. He had big feet, stubble, and dark, curly hair. He definitely needed a haircut, but that, too, was surely part of his presentation of self. He looked mostly clean-cut—I mean, I saw no visible signs of tattoos, no awful pins and needles in his body parts.

I have an old-fashioned revulsion to those pins and needles. One of the waitresses at the coffee house near my office

28

had some sort of metal thing stuck through her tongue. I found it so utterly repulsive that I avoided going there. My favorite waitress, a woman in her 50's whose main sin is a huge mop of hair-sprayed hair, asked me, when I bumped into her on the street, why she never saw me any more, and I told her. "Oh, that was Tiffany," she said. "She was fired."

The new waitress, Tiffany's replacement, had tattoos on her arms. But at least no metal in her tongue. If one of my daughters gets herself pierced, or even tattooed, I honestly don't know what I'd do. I suppose I would survive, but barely.

"Can I come in?" he said. "I've got to talk to you."

"Sure thing," I said. Not that I wanted to talk to him. I had work to do. But I unlocked the door to my office and waved him in. He went in ahead of me. I noticed his jeans were baggy and loose, and hung around his rather narrow hips. The top of his polka dot underwear was plainly visible. I suppose that, too, had become normal. Why they would want to advertise their underwear is another of life's mysteries.

Teddy said, "I got your name from Margot."

I nodded.

"She said I should talk to you. It's about that dead body thing."

I was afraid of that. I said nothing. I didn't want to encourage him in any way. I didn't know Teddy then. He was not easily discouraged. I have to tell you: I came to like him a lot. He looked like the others of his species, but Teddy was smart, and sweet, and resourceful. In a way, he had to be. He was seventeen, the only child of a single mother, and he was basically a nerd. I don't mean that disrespectfully. Nerds are the best people on earth. They do all the creative, interesting things. Jocks accomplish nothing. They swagger about with sawdust in their brains and attract others with similar mental equipment. And then they fizzle out quickly. Or maybe I just hope so. Of course, I'm prejudiced. I'm something of a nerd myself.

On the other hand, have I done anything creative or interesting? A new legal theory, perhaps? No, nothing.

One thing about Teddy was quickly apparent. He loved to

talk. Some teenagers are sullen, and speak only in grunts and monosyllables to adult members of the species. Teddy was not one of those. No grunts, no monosyllables. No shyness, either. It was a nonstop flow of words.

"I was with these friends, my buddies," he said. "Guys at school. My friend Omar. He's a real whiz at music stuff, he plays the trombone. Actually, he plays it night and day. Drives his family crazy. I mean, they're kind of proud of him, but a trombone is pretty noisy, you got to admit. And my friend Buzz. He's Chinese. Well, his dad's Chinese. His name isn't really Buzz, it's something Chinese, and nobody can pronounce it. He's a real genius. Anyway, they're my friends. Most of the kids at school, they're pretty stupid, to be honest. Me, Omar, and Buzz, we're in these advanced placement courses, I mean, most of them. I'm not in the math ones, I don't like math. Buzz, he's good at everything, math, science, history, all of it. Especially math.

"Anyway, we were just talking, kidding around, they know about this thing, you know, the dead body, the one in Margot's house, I mean, it freaked her out completely, can you blame her? And Omar and Buzz, they said, Teddy, let's face it, you're the number one suspect. And I went, 'Get out of here! Me, a suspect? You're out of your minds.' And they said, 'well, we know you wouldn't murder this lady, whoever she is, but Teddy, you're the only one had a key, did somebody ever take the key?' I said, 'No way, I wore the key on a string, like around my neck, I slept with it on, I only took it off when I took a shower,' and they said, 'How often was that?' I mean, they kid me, I don't shower that much, big waste of time, and I never shower in school, like after gym, none of us shower, it's like Omar said, who wants people looking at your dick and that sort of thing? Anyway, I take a shower at home sometimes, and the key's in the bathroom with me, so nobody ever got that key. My mom could have, but she didn't. So that makes me a suspect. I mean, because I had the key. And maybe the cops think I could have given it to some hoodlum, you know?"

"Really, Teddy," I said. "Nobody thinks you did that."

"I mean, Mr. May, I did have the key, right? I mean, like I

said, I'm sort of a suspect. Some people think that's pretty cool. As if I killed that lady. 'Course, the cops, they're used to this kind of thing, and there's a lot of kids my age, real hoodlums, they're in gangs and do all kinds of stuff, and they could kill people. Maybe somebody raped this woman, then they had to kill her, you know, get rid of her before she went to the police, or maybe she was a witness or something. So the cops, they could suspect me. My high school, though, it's different, I mean, no gangs and hoodlums—just kids, like for example my friend Jerry, his dad is an actual accountant, I mean, you can't get more boring than that, even though his dad, I have to admit it, his dad's pretty cool, he even goes hang-gliding on the weekends, and he went trekking in Nepal or wherever those big mountains are, Tibet I guess. And this other guy Dustin, he's in Buzz's class, AP math, and he has the worst acne, but his dad lives in Singapore, and he's been married five times, and has girl friends, one of them's a movie star, anyway, that's what Dustin says. Our high school, I'm not gonna say we're angels, hey, there's stuff going on, like at parties. Dustin gave this party once, his dad's away, I told you that, and his mom, who knows, anyway, she wasn't there, and the police came and broke it up at 3 a.m. But like I said, no gangs, far as I know, and nobody has guns and knives. Well, nobody I know, anyway."

"Teddy," I said, "Like I told you, I'm sure nobody thinks you killed this woman."

"But maybe they think it's my mom. I know she didn't have the key, but the police, they're really suspicious. Of everybody. I mean, who do they see, day in and day out? Criminals. My mom—hey, maybe she did do it. She's pretty fearless, you know? She's terrific. She could do anything. She could kill somebody, I swear, if she thought it was some sort of bad guy."

He paused, and looked at me; and seemed a bit embarrassed. "I'm shooting my mouth off too much," he said, "and you're asking yourself, why did this kid come here, what's this all about. OK: Margot, this thing is really creeping her out, can you blame her? And she told me about you, how you were going to help her, and I thought, I better go to this guy, tell him what

I know. And that's why I'm here. To tell you stuff."

"Tell me 'stuff.' What kind of stuff?"

"Like I said, what I know."

"OK, Teddy: what do you know? You know who did it?"

"No, no, Mr. May. Nothing like that. No idea. But I know who she was, who the dead woman was. I mean, I think so."

"You think you know who she was, Teddy? I mean, how could that be, Teddy? You didn't see the body, did you?"

"Are you kidding? No way. Me look at a dead body? My grampa died last year, mom's dad, we didn't see him much, he was pretty much out of it, you know, senile. It was a regular funeral, the coffin was wide open, and he was lying there, but I wouldn't look. Pretended something. I was embarrassed. I thought, I'm not looking at dead people. Anyway, nobody showed me this dead lady, why should they? I guess they put the body in the morgue or someplace. But look, it's like this. I do stuff for the neighbors, and sometimes I even house-sit. Not just for Margot. People in the neighborhood, they know I do this sort of thing, and I'm reliable, you know? You can trust me. Anyway, one of the neighbors—like I do for Margot—when this neighbor goes away, you know, I take in the mail, water the plants. She's pretty young, I don't know exactly. Lives alone, far as I know. Anyway, she hasn't been home in days. I don't know how long. I ride my bike to school and I go by there and I know she's not there. She didn't say anything to me or my mom, she didn't say she was going away, and that's pretty strange, and like I said, there were newspapers in the driveway and I peeked in the mailbox and it was full of mail.

"So when I came back from school, I mentioned this, and Mom said, 'She must be away, Teddy, put the newspapers in her garage,' it's not locked, she doesn't lock the garage. Anyway, Mom said, put the mail there too. Mom knows this woman, and, like I said, she's a neighbor. And I was thinking, this is pretty weird. When she goes away, she usually tells my mom, and she talks to me, and gives me instructions, tells me which plants to water, you know, like, 'don't bother with the cactus plant,' and this and that about the mail, that sort of stuff. But she didn't say anything. She's just gone. And she's pretty young,

I don't know, maybe in her 20's, and I know her. I mean, she fits the description. I hate to think she's dead, but maybe she's the one."

I have to admit, this story caught my attention. Could Teddy be on to something?

"The house is right around the corner from us," he said. "Kind of looks the same. Looks a lot like Margot's house, too. Her first name, it'll come to me, it slipped my mind, anyway her last name is King. She works at Stanford; she's a secretary to some big-shot professor. Psychology or something. Does big experiments. We read about him in school, in social science. Anyway, when she goes away, she leaves a key with my mom. She says, in case of emergency, it's a good idea to leave a key with a neighbor. Our key, we leave it with the people on the other side, the Dobbs family. We've got a burglar alarm too. Pain in the butt, if you ask me. But anyway, this Miss King, she doesn't go away much, maybe once a year, but when she's gone, like with Margot, I have to do stuff. Feed the cat—only the cat died, so I don't have to do that anymore—but I could still take in the mail, that sort of thing. So where'd she go? And she's young, and ... you know what I'm saying, Mr. May? I think she could be the dead woman."

I felt excited. This did sound like a genuine lead. A young woman, living not far from Margot Williams—and she seemed to be gone. And her behavior was unusual. She never told Teddy's mother she was going, which seemed odd. I had to ask: "When did this woman leave?"

"I don't know. Like I said, she never told us."

"Did you tell this to the police, Teddy?"

"The police? No way. I don't want anything to do with police. I'm telling *you*, Mr. May. I think we should do something, the two of us. Like Margot said, this is sort of a hobby of yours, I mean, solving stuff. So I thought, this is important, I've got a real clue, I better tell you. That's what Margot thought, too."

"I think you should tell the police," I said. "I'm not the right person, Teddy."

"Look," he said, "my mom has the key to the house. I know where it is. The house, it's real close by. I say, let's go there and look around. Maybe she left a clue, or wrote something, or ... I don't know. What's the harm? We just want to look around."

I said, "You know, Teddy, we shouldn't do this. It's none of your business, and it's none of my business. I'm not going to go there, if that's what you're asking."

But Teddy said, "Well, I'm going to go, anyway. Honestly, Mr. May, there's no harm done. I mean, there's nobody there. It's all dark, and like I told you, I put the newspapers in the garage, and the mail. I didn't want burglars to see the stuff, they might think, hey, nobody's home, I can break in there. The point is, she could be the one, the one in Margot's house. I mean, I'd hate to think she's dead, but it's somebody, isn't it? And we wouldn't be doing anything wrong. I'd just go in, look around. Maybe she needs me to water the plants, you know?"

"Okay, Teddy: I think you shouldn't do it. But that's your business. I'm not going."

"Oh, you got to, Mr. May. I mean, you're doing the investigating, so, you have to be along. I mean, you're an expert ..."

I had a feeling it would be useless to issue the usual set of denials: there was no help for it. I was Frank May, the great detective. I sighed, and said, "OK Teddy, investigating stuff, let's say it's my hobby. It isn't, but let's say it is. So this woman is, well, missing, this woman, Miss King."

"I just remembered her first name. Lissa. She's Lissa King."

"OK, so she's not around, and the mail is piling up; you could be right, Teddy. But it's the police who have to get this information. It's got nothing to do with me. Or us."

But Teddy Gilchrist ignored my comment. He smelled an adventure. "Mr. May," he said, "it's not like we're doing anything wrong. Like I said, she leaves a key with my mom, in case. I know where Mom keeps it. She keeps it under a flowerpot. I'll just get it, and we'll take a look, I mean, what's the harm?"

"'Take a look,' Teddy? We have no right to go rummaging around in somebody's house."

"Well, sure," he said, "but we've got the key, right? And maybe my mom said, Teddy, here's the key. Miss King, she's gone somewhere, I guess she forgot to tell us she was going, and you better go water the plants."

"But she didn't say that, Teddy, did she?"

"No, but she could have. What do you say? Omar and Buzz, I told them about this, and they said, go for it. It's not like it's dangerous or anything. And we're helping people out, I mean, the police."

"It's not a good idea, Teddy. You could get into trouble."

"Not if you come with me. I mean, you're a lawyer, right?"

"I am a lawyer, Teddy. Not a criminal lawyer, though. But let me tell you something, you're not supposed to search somebody's house. Not without a warrant. The police, they have to have a warrant, signed by a judge. Otherwise, it's illegal."

"Mr. May, we're not searching. We're just watering the plants. I did this before. She's got some nice plants. A great big one, in the living room, she loves that plant, it's really big. She went on vacation last summer, and I had to water the darn thing. It's in a great big pot. So that's my excuse. But you've gotta come with me, in case I find clues."

"Clues, Teddy? We're looking for clues?"

I could see, there was no way to talk him out of it. He was bubbling over with excitement. This was a lot better than AP Social Studies, which he was cutting at this very moment, as he admitted to me later on. I kept protesting for a while, but in the end, against my better judgment, I agreed to go with him. Better judgments never win. "But I won't go in," I said. "You can go in and water the plants; I'll wait outside; and you can tell me if you saw something, or found something, OK?"

Teddy, I'm sure, would have preferred if the great detective came with him to the house. But he had to settle for my proposal. I really had no idea what he thought he would find.

We fixed on a time, after school. I picked him up at Gunn High School, in Palo Alto, and we drove to the house. It was late afternoon.

It was a very ordinary looking house, almost a cottage. Two stories, but rather low-slung. There was not much you could tell from the street. The house was set back from the line of the sidewalk, and there was a row of hedges, which I was grateful for; I could stand inside the property line, just behind the hedge and I would be practically invisible from the street. I kept saying to myself, why am I doing this? Teddy was chattering away as we drove. I barely listened.

I parked, and stationed myself. Teddy, who had the key, went inside the house. I stood behind the hedge, watching the traffic go by. I thought to myself, what a fool's errand this is, and how did I ever allow myself to be talked into it? A half hour or so went by. I was sorry I hadn't brought a book to read. Then the door opened, and Teddy said, "Bingo, Mr. May, I think I found something."

"What is it?"

"Come on in, I'll show you."

I followed him inside and closed the door. He led me past a rather drab living room. There was, indeed, an enormous plant, some palm-like specimen of botanical majesty, with a thick stem, and dark leaves, growing almost as high as the ceiling. We went into a bedroom. Again, nothing special. There was a double bed, with a pink bedspread, two ordinary pillows, and three or four decorative pillows, in rather garish colors. Across the room was a dresser, with brushes and combs on top, along with a few boxes, which I suppose contained cosmetics, or costume jewelry, or whatever. There was a closet, and a small bathroom off to the side. On the bed was an open suitcase, but it was empty.

"Don't you see?" Teddy said, in an eager tone of voice.

"See what?"

"That suitcase. I mean, it's a real clue. Look, she was planning to go someplace. But she never got to go. Somebody came in, and grabbed her. Maybe somebody she knew. I mean, she opened the door for them. I think she was scared, she knew they were after her; that's why she wanted to get the hell out of here. But she never had a chance."

"Teddy," I said, "you've got a vivid imagination. Just because there's this open suitcase, you're making a whole Sherlock Holmes thing out of it."

"Yeah, but it makes sense, doesn't it? She's not here, right?

She's missing. She was planning to go somewhere, right? She got out this suitcase, but she never got around to packing it ... I wish I could tell if her clothes are all still here, you know what I'm saying? I mean, isn't that what happened? And then ..."

He never finished the sentence. We heard something that sent chills down my spine. The sound of a key, then the sound of the door as it opened. "Shit," Teddy said. "Somebody's here, we got to hide."

I had no intention of hiding, and besides, there wasn't time. In a few second, I saw a young, blonde woman, standing in the doorway of the bedroom. "Jesus," Teddy said, "It's her."

She was staring at us. Then she said, "Teddy Gilchrist, what on earth are you doing here? And who is this guy?"

I guess she wasn't dead after all.

5

The whole situation was profoundly embarrassing, as you can imagine. I was speechless. But Teddy was equal to the task. "Hi Miss King" he said, bold as brass, "I saw you weren't around, and the mail was kind of piling up, and stuff, so I took the key and thought I'd water your plants, bring in the mail, that sort of thing. Isn't that OK?"

"I don't know. I never asked you ... but I guess you meant well. But who is this man?"

I should have answered. I should have said something, but I was tongue-tied, my feeble brain working hard to think up some excuse.

"He's Frank May," Teddy said, "I just asked him to come along."

"You asked him? But why?"

Teddy shrugged his shoulders. I could almost see the gears in his brain whirling, just like mine were, looking for some sort of excuse. He never found a good one. "No particular reason," he said, edging himself—and me—toward the door. She stood there staring at us as we beat a hasty retreat.

* * *

I went home, terribly ashamed of myself. How did I ever get dragged into this sort of thing? Teddy had convinced me that this King woman was dead, and that her body had been the one in Margot's house. This seemed quite plausible to me, but Lissa King was very much alive, as it turned out. We had had the bad luck of rummaging around in her house at precisely the wrong time—the exact moment she came back from wherever she was. And then only to discover Teddy Gilchrist and some stranger in her bedroom!

By the time I got home, it was dark. The girls were gone at a friend's house, or so they said. You never know if they're telling the truth. Celia was in the living room, knitting a sweater. "It's for Adam," she said. That would be Adam Finkel, who taught math at Celia's high school. Adam, a very shy man in his forties, has a terrible skin problem: all bumps and boils on his face. High school kids can be merciless. They call him Dr. Frankenstein.

In fact, he's sweet, in spite of being bumbling and ineffectual. He's single (of course), and lives with his crotchety and extremely elderly mother. Celia has taken a real liking to Adam, and she invites him over whenever she sees a chance of achieving one of her goals in life: finding him a woman. Maybe she thought a new sweater might do the trick. Alas, what he needed was some sort of surgery, but apparently no dermatologist had ever succeeded in dealing with his problem. Perhaps the best alternative would be a mask, something like the Phantom of the Opera.

"Where were you, Frank? I thought you'd be home early tonight."

"I was at a client's house," I said. I hate telling lies. I told myself I'd tell her the truth later, explain, and apologize. But the situation was too raw for me to go into at the moment. I felt wounded and humiliated. I changed the subject, as adroitly as I could. I felt like an utter fool. And bone-tired. We ate leftovers, watched a mindless program on TV, and went to bed.

* * *

The next day, Teddy showed up at my office, just after lunch. "Hey, Teddy," I said, "shouldn't you be in school?"

"Yeah. I should. But I skipped it today. I mean, I went there in the morning. Afternoon class, I can't stand it. We're doing some really dumb stuff. AP History, I mean, I like history, honestly I do, wars and so on, but this is about the constitutional convention, and it's so boring. George Washington and Jefferson and Madison and all of those guys, we had to read the Federalist Papers, I mean, they're classics I guess, but who wants to read them? And the teacher, Miss Mitnick, she loves the stuff, we had to pretend to be founding fathers or something, she'd say, you get to be Jefferson or Madison, and talk about Article II or was it Article III, and I thought, 'I'm not gonna play these games, screw Jefferson,' pardon me, so I said, 'Miss Mitnick, I have a terrible headache,' and she said, 'A headache?' And I said, 'Yes, it's a migraine.' I mean, I don't even know what that is, but my Aunt Jenny always complains about migraines, and she said, 'Well, okay,' and I skipped out, got my bike and here I am. Day off wouldn't hurt me. And I needed to talk to you."

"Teddy, what about? I'm really busy."

But he settled down in a chair, and kept right on talking. "Hey, that was awful yesterday, really embarrassing. But, you know, I'm glad. I mean, glad she isn't dead. She's really nice. Pretty too. She's got some bosom on her, did you notice?"

"Hey, Teddy," I said, "I'm a middle-aged, married man. I'm not supposed to notice bosoms."

"Aw, come on, you saw them, I know you did."

In fact, I had. Lissa King was attractive, somewhat buxom, and was wearing a tight blouse. But the last thing on my mind, in that situation, was sexual fantasy.

Teddy went on, "Anyway, I figured, I better talk to her. I mean, I didn't want her blabbing to my mom, telling her, you know, 'Teddy was in my house with some guy. What was that all about?' So I got on my bike and went back there and rang the doorbell, and she came out and I said, 'Miss King, I need to apologize.' And she said, 'Boy, do you ever, and you better tell me what you were up to, and who that guy was, the one with you. I mean, if I didn't know Teddy Gilchrist, I'd think someone was trying to rob me.' And I went, 'Gee Miss King, I'd never do that, I'm an honest kid, you know me, believe me, I'd never take advantage, honest to God.' Then I said, 'Can I come in and talk to you? It won't take long.'"

"I take it she let you in. What did you say?"

"I gave her a new line of bull. I said, 'Miss King, I told you a lie, I wasn't watering plants, maybe I should of, but the truth is, I was worried about you, I mean, you were gone, I mean, the mail was piling up, and the newspaper, and I was wondering, maybe she's sick or something, or stuff.' And I said, 'Remember what happened last year, I mean, that old guy, Gustav Schmidt, the one who lived down the block, grumpy old man, he was a million years old, and the mail was piling up, and finally somebody went in, and he was lying on the floor, had a heart attack or something, and he was dead, and maybe he didn't die right away, and if somebody went in, they could've saved him?'"

"And she believed you?"

"Hey, who knows? I don't think so. She was, well, skeptical. She said, 'Teddy, that's ridiculous, I remember that business with Gustav, but he was 93 years old and I'm not. And who was that guy?' And I said, 'His name is Frank May, and he's a lawyer.' And she says, 'A lawyer? What did you need a lawyer for?' And I went, 'No, I didn't need a lawyer, but he's also some kind of investigator, and my mom knows him, and Margot and Jim Williams, they know him, and some of the neighbors, and, well, it's because we were worried, did something happen to you, that's why I wanted him along, honest to God.'"

"And she believed *that* story?"

"I think she kind of did. But she said, 'He's an investigator, but what was he investigating? You mean he's a private detective?' And I said, well, sort of ..."

I groaned, "oh my God."

Teddy ignored this. He went right on, "'Well, if you were a missing person, that sort of thing.' But I didn't want her asking too many questions, so I turned the tables on her, and I started asking questions. I said, 'Miss King, OK, maybe we did the wrong thing, but we were worried, like I said, like, did something happen? And we didn't know where you were, and you didn't say anything, like you usually do, you know, water the plants and stuff. I mean, obviously, you were away. Where did you go?'"

"And what did she say?"

"She just said, 'Don't ask me. I had things I had to take care of.' So I said, 'Yeah, like what? Miss King, remember, we were thinking of you, I mean, worrying about you.' But she didn't tell me. Then she says, 'Anyway, why were the two of you in the bedroom?' And I said, 'Well, we were looking all over the house, and then there was the suitcase, the open suitcase, that seemed awfully funny, why was there an open suitcase, like you started to pack, and then got interrupted.'"

"And what did she say then?"

"She said, 'Teddy, you've got a vivid imagination. You're right; I did go on a trip. And I took out that suitcase, but then I realized I didn't need a big suitcase, so I grabbed an overnight bag, and that's what I took along. And I was in a hurry, so I just left the suitcase there, on the bed. Little did I think,' she said, 'that people would be rummaging around in the house, making up stories about that suitcase.' And I said, 'Gee, Miss King, I'm really truly sorry, and it won't happen again, and really, I was just thinking about you and worrying.' And then I went home."

He seemed quite pleased with himself. As for me ... but there's no point in fighting the ridiculous notion that I'm some sort of private eye. So I just said, "Thanks for telling me. I'm glad you did what you did. But now, let's just forget all about it. It's over. End of story."

But it wasn't the end. It was just the beginning.

6

My involvement—involvement I never expected to have—began two days later. I had spent a useful morning working on documents for a client, and then treated myself to a terrific Chinese lunch at the Golden Dragon, right down the street from my office. When I came back, I was hoping to shut the door to my office, slump in my seat, and have a brief but delicious nap. Instead, I found a woman waiting for me. I recognized Lissa King. She was wearing a pale pink blouse and black slacks. She seemed distraught and her blonde hair was a bit disheveled.

I have to admit, despite what I told Teddy, that I had noticed her figure. Of course, the situation had been embarrassing and I hadn't looked at her that closely. Now that she was in front of me, I saw how attractive she really was. Even though she seemed distressed.

"I've been waiting a long time," she said. "I was just about to give up. I've got to see you, Mr. May."

"Of course," I said. "And do call me Frank."

"You can call me Lissa." She sat down on the chair in my office. She looked as if she had been crying. I began by apologizing for the intrusion. I repeated the story Teddy had told her, about people worrying because she was obviously away and had not done what she usually did when she was on a trip. She waved one of her hands dismissively. She obviously did not believe this story, but was not about to argue. Not at the moment.

"Please," she said. "I have to talk to you. But I can't stay long; I have to get back to work. I work at Stanford, in the psych department. I'm an assistant to a professor."

I nodded my head.

"The man I work for is Ramsey Hardcastle. He's a famous man, a big person in the field of psychology. That's not the reason why I'm here, it's something else."

Her boss's name was vaguely familiar. Then I remembered: he was Sylvan's client. Later on, I would be sorry I ever heard the name.

"The real reason I'm here," she said, "is because of my sister."

"Your sister?"

"My sister Geena." She choked up, and began to cry. "My poor sister."

"Your sister ... is she, well, sick?"

"She's dead, Frank."

"I'm awfully sorry. How, uh, how did it happen?"

"Somebody killed her."

"My God. That's so awful. I'm terribly, terribly sorry."

"The other day, when I came home and ... and Teddy asked me where I had gone, I didn't answer. But I had gone to look for my sister. She was missing, I mean, I didn't know where she was. I went to L.A. to look for her. That's where she used to live, so I thought, maybe that's where she might be. I couldn't find any trace of her. Then I came back and ... and you were in the house, and I didn't know why. But now I know."

"Now you know?"

"I read something in the paper, and ... oh God ... I hoped it wasn't her ... this woman, this dead woman, it was so strange, she was in somebody's house, in a cedar chest, the body ... I thought, please God, not Geena, please God. She ran away with some guy, that must be it. But it was Geena; I had this feeling in the pit of my stomach. I called the police. I had to identify her. I broke down, I really did, when I saw her in the morgue—my poor sister. It was the most awful day of my life."

She began crying again. I handed her a tissue. I keep them on my desk, for clients who cry, or who have sinus infections.

"I have to tell you the whole story," she said. "Well, as much of it as I know. There are three of us, three sisters. My dad was married twice, his first wife divorced him. They had a daughter, she lives in Cincinnati. Then Dad married again—my mother—he was way older than she was, they had two daughters, Geena and me. Mom got breast cancer and died when I was still pretty little, a first grader. Geena was two years older, and Dad, he was an old man, and he couldn't handle us, so we were separated. She went to an aunt in Los Angeles, and I went to another aunt, in San Francisco. So there was a long time when I didn't see much of Geena. I didn't know anything about her life and she was always very private, always full of secrets, even when we were little girls. Well, we grew up, went to high school, then college, and I knew she was in Los Angeles. She had her own apartment by then, and we saw each other, oh, maybe once a year. I got married, it didn't last long, but I had my own life to live, and Geena wasn't part of it. Geena got married, too, but that broke up. I guess both of us aren't good with men ... Oh God, she's dead, and she'll never have a chance ..."

I sat there silently. She was sobbing uncontrollably. I waited a few minutes. She said, "I'm sorry. I just ... I can't control myself."

"Don't worry," I said. "This must be terribly hard for you."

"You can't believe how hard ... Anyway," she said, going on with her story, "about, well, six months ago I think it was, Geena suddenly appeared on my doorstep. I mean, literally. No call, no letter, no warning. She drove up from L.A. She said she had to get away from things, and I'm sure it must have been some guy, but I didn't ask, and she didn't tell. She moved in— I've got the space, you saw my house, my aunt left it to me when she died. It's got an extra bedroom. Geena told me she had her things in the car and she just went out and brought them in, two big suitcases. I asked her, 'What about your house in L.A., your furniture?' She said she sold everything. She said she'd look for a job, and a place to live—she didn't want to impose on me—but I guess she didn't find a job. And I liked having her around. I didn't ask her for rent. She was still awfully private, in some ways like a stranger, but I don't have much in the way of family, and she was my sister, and I always wanted to be close to her. I sort of loved her. I did love her. We didn't talk much and she kept pretty much to herself, but she was still family, and I wanted to throw my arms around her and hug her. I'm so sorry I didn't. Now I'll never have the chance, she's gone, gone forever ...

"You see, she disappeared suddenly. Well, not exactly. She said she was going away. 'Just for a day,' she said. I said, 'Sure, fine Geena, whatever you want. Where are you going?' But she wouldn't say. It was some sort of secret. She got in her car, and drove off. But then she didn't come back, and I got panicky. Her clothes were still in the house, it's not like she had moved out—her toothbrush was still in her bathroom—I mean, she just didn't come back. I told my boss I needed some time off, though he hates it when I even miss a day. I had to do it. I thought, I'll go to L.A., talk to my aunt, find out things ... I thought she might have gone back there, I thought maybe there was a guy in the picture, maybe even her ex-husband. We've got a cousin there, too, that's where I stayed. Actually, my mother's cousin, Bessie. She hadn't seen or heard from my sister. My Aunt Mona, she's the one Geena lived with, as a kid, well, Aunt Mona had no idea. That's the way Geena was. Secretive, very independent."

"Did she have friends in L.A.? People who knew her?"

"Geena was always a loner. I told you she was married once. Didn't last long. He was some kind of businessperson. His name was Logan Manning. Wasn't a happy marriage. I barely knew him. They got divorced."

"Did you look him up? I imagine the police must have questioned him. Ex-husband. Bitter, maybe. That's often ... well, the one."

"Oh, Logan, sure, he could be bitter. He was bitter. I never liked him, not that I saw him that often. He seemed sullen, maybe even violent; I guess I shouldn't say things like that. Geena never complained, but she got rid of him. Or he got rid of her, I don't know. Anyway, he's not involved in this. Believe me, the police did check him out. He moved to Atlanta, got married again, that marriage didn't work out either, and now he's living with some girlfriend, still in Atlanta, and he was there the whole time, went to work, did things, no, he's not the one. No way he could have done this awful thing."

"Boyfriends, though?"

"I did talk to one woman in L.A. She worked with Geena and used to have lunch with her. I happened to know her name, from something Geena said. I looked her up and talked to her. Said she thought Geena maybe did have a boyfriend. But she wasn't sure. Geena just didn't like to talk about things like that. This woman had no idea who this boyfriend was, or even his name, or anything. Anyway, Geena quit her job very suddenly and moved up here. This woman said she was really surprised at that ... maybe Geena had a reason; she didn't know."

"And you didn't know either, why she came up here? She never talked to you about it?"

"No. Not at all. You know, Frank, I think it was a wild goose chase, I mean, me going to Los Angeles. She wasn't there. Or, if she had been there, she didn't let anyone know. You know what I think? I think she never left town. I think I was looking in the wrong place. I think she was here the whole time. But where, and with whom, I have no idea. Anyway, I was worried, really worried. Then I came back, and ... and you and Teddy were in the house. And then I read about the dead girl ... well, you know the rest."

I said something sympathetic. At least we knew who the dead woman was. But why was Lissa here? What did she want from me? I was afraid of what was coming.

"I know you're investigating this case ..."

Oh God. Not that. "No, no ..."

"People say you are. And that's fine, Frank," she said. "I want to know everything. How did you know it was Geena? How did you know it was my sister?"

"Lissa, I knew absolutely nothing."

"That can't be right. It's why you came to my house, isn't it? You knew—or you thought you knew—it was Geena, and you wanted to see. To look for leads, I don't know what, but it's natural, you'd have to see the place. And Teddy had the key ..."

"No, Lissa, no: I swear it."

She burst into tears. "Please help me, Frank. I'm so unhappy. Why would somebody do this to Geena? My poor sister. People say you're a good person. And smart. Promise you'll help."

How could I say no? "Lissa, I'm not what you think, I'm not a detective."

"Help me," she said, "I don't care what you are, just help me. You can do it, everybody says so."

I resisted, feebly, but ultimately felt there was no point. I kept thinking that the police would probably arrest somebody soon. They usually do. Any day now, they'll crack the case wide open. Then I'll be off the hook.

"Oh, thank you, Frank," she said. "I'm so terribly grateful." And she hugged me before she left. It was a very substantial hug and I felt the pressure of her body, including that very substantial bosom.

I sat there after she was gone. I would have liked to help her. But I had no idea how.

7

I put the matter out of my mind. I had made a promise, but I had no intention of keeping it. None whatsoever. But fate had different plans for me.

The very next day, I had a visit from another very unhappy woman, Margot Williams. She brought Jim.

"I took the day off," she said. "I just can't function. Frank, it's driving me crazy. I made poor Jim come with me. The police questioned us again. Both of us together, and then separately. Really. They can't get the idea out of their heads that we somehow knew this woman. They know who she is now. Her name is Geena King. They keep trying to find a connection. And there isn't, I swear it. We weren't even here at the time. We were miles and miles away. Anyway, I have to tell you something. I'm pregnant. Three months pregnant. That's why we took the trip, sort of a last fling ... you know, a baby, it makes a huge difference, and you can't live the way you're used to. Anyway, we went. It seemed like such a good idea, and we had such a good time, until ..."

Tears started flowing. I handed her a tissue. Jim looked uncomfortable. She said to him, "I'll talk to Frank, is that okay? You don't have to stay. Pick me up downstairs, on the corner, in an hour. I know you wanted to look for a new tennis racket at that sports store."

He kissed her and left. Margot said, "Did you know, this poor woman—the dead woman—she was pregnant too? I keep thinking: I'm unhappy right now, stressed, because of this awful thing ... but I'm going to have a baby, I'm so happy about that. And here she's dead, she'll never be a mother. God, the things that come into my mind. If only the police would stop bothering us."

"What do they want?" I said. "They know you two weren't even here at the time, you were a hundred miles away."

"Oh, I think they're just floundering. They seem totally baffled. But, you know, Jim and I both lived in Los Angeles. That's where we met, that's where we got married. I think that's why they keep pestering us—this Geena woman lived in Los Angeles. God, so do millions of people! Neither of us knew her from Adam. My company, the one I worked for at the time, had an office in Los Angeles, and I thought, hey, why not, I mean, when they asked me if I would like to transfer to L.A., at least for some months—and I did. I had some college friends there, and I met Jim at a party. An old friend of mine lived in Echo Park and she gave this party, and this friend, Rosalind was her name, she said, 'Margot, I'd like you to meet somebody,' and there was Jim, and I thought he was a good-looking guy. We started talking, and well, somehow we clicked, and I started seeing him, and he came to my place, and one thing led to another ... we were really attracted to each other and I ended up pregnant. Jim ... to be honest, he didn't want the baby, he said he wasn't ready to settle down, but I said, 'Well, I'm having this baby,' and we talked and talked, had serious discussions, and the upshot was we got married and moved up here. As you know, I had a house here—I inherited it, I told you that—and we moved in, and Jim and I got jobs at Stanford ..."

"And the baby?"

"No baby, not that time. I had a miscarriage. But we were married, after all, and I loved him. And I think he loved me. I mean, I know he does. No complaints. And now he does want a baby, just like I do ... and I'm very happy about this baby. Very happy. Life seemed just about perfect. That is, until this awful thing happened."

"And there really is no connection at all, between you and this Geena?"

"I mean, how could there be? We never laid eyes on her. They kept after Jim, asking questions just because he lived in the same city as this woman. And me, too, because I was there, and there is, after-all, a connection—but it's so flimsy, it's laughable. First of all, I work at Stanford and this woman, Geena, lived with her sister, and her sister works at Stanford. So do ten thousand other people. So what kind of connection is that? And then, there's Teddy Gilchrist. He waters the plans for us when we go away, and for that other house too. That makes the police so suspicious! As if that's some sort of real connection, or a motive for killing somebody. I mean, it's ridiculous. But they won't let go. It's ridiculous, but it's driving me crazy."

I made sympathetic clicking noises.

"But that's not what I want to talk to you about. We want to ask you about estate planning ... we've been talking, me and Jim. You know, it's tough, sharing a life. We've had a few rough patches, I guess everybody does, but I think we're over that. To be honest, I've thought sometimes that maybe it wouldn't last—now I just know it will. This baby, our baby, it wasn't exactly planned—you know, sometimes these things just happen—but I'm really happy about it. Really happy. Excited, actually. And Jim is excited too."

"That's great news, Margot," I said. Actually, my mind was a million miles away. I was wearing a pair of new shoes, and one of them was pinching the toes on my left foot. I was hoping Margot would leave, so that I could take the damn shoe off and give my poor toes a rest. But she went right on talking.

"I mean, it was something of a shock, the pregnancy—a shock for Jim—that's what I'm talking about. He's afraid he's not ready. To be a father. I mean, he *was* afraid. Now I think it's okay. He felt that way the last time too; and when I had the miscarriage, he was secretly relieved. He didn't say so, but I could tell, and I was upset, and I didn't think *he* was upset—we had a huge argument. But that's all gone. I know he'll be an amazing daddy, he's a very emotional man, he doesn't show it sometimes, but he is. And I really love him."

My toes were killing me.

"The baby's changed things," she said. "I'm going to quit my job in couple of months. I want to be a stay-at-home mother. Or try it anyway. And since I'm pregnant, don't you think we need a will in case something happens to us? I mean, nothing's going to happen, but I read this magazine article that said everybody should have a will. And our house is worth a fortune. I looked it up on that website, you know the one, and it said our house is worth $2,000,000. Can you imagine? How can anybody afford a house around here? I know we couldn't, if we had to start from scratch. And it's my house, it's all mine, and not even a mortgage, because I got it from my aunt when she died. Jim has some money, too, from savings. And there's the money I got from my grandmother ... I mean, Frank, don't you agree that we should make some plans? Do we need separate wills, me and Jim?"

We spent some time talking about wills, trusts, the probate process, and estate planning in general. She listened carefully. I told her, yes; she and Jim should have separate wills. I told her about how they could avoid probate costs with a living trust. I also gently explained my fees. She said she would talk to Jim. "I mean, it has to be a joint decision, doesn't it? But he'll do what you suggest, I just know it. We'll set something up for the baby, like you mentioned." I gave her a memo about living trusts (actually, I copied it from a manual) and told her to read it and then get back to me. And I would be happy to talk to Jim, of course. Then she left.

* * *

I told Celia about this conversation. She said, "Frank, that's fine. She could be a good client—they've got some money, and with the baby and all, yes, they do need your services. All fine and dandy. But you're not going to get involved in the murder thing, are you?"

"No way, honey," I said. "This is business. Regular business. Estate planning. It's what I do. It has nothing to do with the murder. I'm not involved in that at all."

But there I was wrong.

8

I had not dismissed from my mind—I have to admit it—the puzzling and mysterious death of Geena King. At odd moments, leaning back in my chair, taking a mental break from some document I was drafting or reading, the thing came swimming into my brain, and made me wonder—what could it mean? Why would somebody kill this woman, and dump her in Margot Williams' house while she and her husband were away? Why indeed? And how?

Teddy Gilchrist was also thinking about this affair. Clearly he found it terrifically exciting. "Hey, maybe I'm going to solve this case," he said. He had the habit of showing up at my office at odd hours. He rode over on his bike from high school. I said, "Teddy, you're cutting too many classes."

"Doesn't matter," he said. "I got my SAT scores, and they're awesome. Better than Omar, by ten points. I told him, 'I'm smarter than you, Omar. It's a scientific fact.' He said, 'Yeah, maybe, but don't forget, I can beat the shit out of you.' He was just joking. I mean, he could, if he wanted to, you should see the muscles on that guy. But he wouldn't, we're buddies. Buzz, he did better than both of us on these tests. Gets these fantastic math scores. I can't compete with that guy."

He told me he had skipped AP History. Again. I said, "Teddy, it's a bad idea. And you should know something about our history. You really should."

He said, "Hey, maybe. But the teacher, she's a total dork. I read the textbook, so I don't need the stupid class. She's always going on and on about the founding fathers, I mean, who cares?

She gets all starry-eyed about Thomas Jefferson, can you believe it? I said to her, 'Well, he was having an affair with a slave woman,' and she got huffy, and said, 'That isn't relevant Mr. Gilchrist, his personal life is not important, his political contributions, however ...' Blah blah. She doesn't like me, but I ace the quizzes, so she can't say anything. Anyway, I had a breakthrough on the case. Something new. A real development."

I told him I didn't want to hear about any breakthroughs, and he should stay out of it; it was a matter for the police. Period. Any breakthroughs were for the police to make. But of course, when I said I didn't want to hear about breakthroughs, I was lying. I did want to hear. Anyway, as I expected, he ignored my protests.

"Guess what, Mr. May. We found the car."

"What car?"

"Geena's car. It's parked on the street, oh, about a block from Lissa's house, around the corner. Just sitting there. But here's what's weird. It wasn't there before. Honest to God. I mean, I go by there every day on my way to school. I swear it. That car wasn't there. Now it is."

"Teddy, you can't really be sure."

"Man, I'm sure. I asked Lissa, 'What kind of a car did your sister have?' She said, 'It's a green Camry hybrid.' I know the car. My uncle Jesse has one, gets great gas mileage, and he's got the same color, some kind of puke green. I asked him, 'Uncle Jesse, why did you get a car with that color? It's a terrible color!' and he said, 'It was cheap, it was the last car on the lot and they wanted to get rid of it.' I said, 'I'll bet they did.' So ... I mean, Mr. May, you have to believe me. That car wasn't there. The day after the murder, it wasn't there. Somebody drove it there and parked it later on. The guy who killed her, that's who it must have been. So this is a clue, a big clue."

"OK, Teddy," I said. "Let's assume it's a clue. But we're not looking for clues, are we? The police, they're looking for clues. We're minding our own business."

I felt as if I was channeling Celia at that moment. She would have said, in no uncertain terms, that it was none of my business. Or Teddy's. Margot and Jim were clients. I could write a will for them, I could get them a living trust, and I could refer them to a personal injury lawyer if somebody backed into their car in some parking lot, but solving the murder of Geena King—no way.

Teddy was disappointed, of course. I think he expected me to get all excited, maybe rush out of the office to investigate the mysterious green Camry hybrid. I did nothing of the sort. But after he left, I did start thinking. If he was right—and Teddy was the sort of person who that was right about things like that—then his information *was* important. And mysterious. Where did this car fit in? Who drove it, and why? Was she murdered in that car? Many questions, no answers. Yet.

* * *

Lissa called me the next day. I asked her whether there was any progress in the case. She said, "No, not as far as I know. I've heard nothing. I suppose they're investigating, but maybe I'd be the last to know."

"I'm sure there'll be some sort of break," I said. Of course, I wasn't sure at all. But poor Lissa was so miserable. "Frank," she said, "I can't stand the idea, that somebody's out there, some awful, terrible human being, somebody who killed my poor sister. I can't sleep at night, I keep thinking about her. And there's nothing I can do about it. Frank, I had her cremated. I know she wanted that. I didn't want to do it, but I did."

I expressed my sympathy again.

"People have been wonderful," she said. "Neighbors. My aunt came up from L.A. and she was so helpful. Tina Gilchrist, she's been wonderful too. Keeps inviting me over, says I shouldn't be alone, and she wants to feed me, she's always making things for me to eat—as if I was hungry. Well, actually, I am. Then there's my job. I think I'd go crazy if I didn't go to work. I wake up, I don't want to get out of bed, but I know I have to. I drag myself to work. But actually, it's my salvation. Dora—she's the Chairman's assistant—she's been so sweet. The job: actually, that's why I called."

"About your job?"

"I think I mentioned, Frank, that I work for a Professor in the Psych Department. His name is Ramsey Hardcastle. He's quite a famous man in his field, has an honorary degree from some school in Sweden and all kinds of awards, though he's not exactly an easy person to work for. Well, anyway, he asked me to call you and set up an appointment with him."

"Me? He asked for me?"

"Well, you're Frank May, aren't you?"

"I am, Lissa. Of course. But what's this all about?"

"To be honest, I have no idea. He didn't tell me. I suppose something legal; you're a lawyer, after all."

I found this odd. Why would this famous professor, who surely had a lawyer—probably someone at a big firm, like Wilson Soncini, or Ropes and Gray—why would he want to see me, of all people? I don't want to undersell myself, but it did seem strange. If he wanted a will or a living trust, there were plenty of highly regarded firms that could do that for him. At any rate, Lissa and I did set up the appointment. It took some doing, and a number of phone calls. This juggling was necessary because the professor, as Lissa told me, was "a very busy man."

I looked him up on the internet. To be exact, I googled him. I found quite a lot of information about Ramsey Hardcastle, the Reginald and Fiona Barfuss Professor of Psychology. He was indeed a famous man in his field. Innovative, bold in his research. Famous—and, to a degree, infamous. He was especially well known for a series of studies in which he induced anger in children. These came to be known as "studies of young wrath," or "studies of unmanaged anger." There were parallel studies in which he induced cruelty in children, though, in fairness, he also studied ways to induce empathy.

No university or government agency would allow such studies today, and they would never get past the Institutional Review Board. You had to wonder how Hardcastle managed to get permission, even when he did these studies, some fifteen to twenty years ago—if indeed he had permission. The whole thing was very controversial. The basic idea of these studies was to set up situations in which young kids, eight to ten years old, would be given tasks. The trick was, the tasks seemed easy, but they were manipulated to make them actually impossible in order to create more and more anger and frustration in the kids. He wanted to know how they would react. Would they lash out at each other? How would they handle toys? Would they smash them to bits? That sort of thing.

Later, he did studies called the "guardian" studies, in which kids were asked to play a game. The winner of the game (which the researchers manipulated) would have the right either to punish the loser, or to get a piece of candy. An astonishing number of kids chose to punish the losers—by spanking them on their butts—rather than get the candy. Maybe it wasn't the right kind of candy. Hardcastle's articles were considered minor classics, especially his case studies of two of the kids, whom he called "Little Willie" and "Little Anna," and who reacted in rather extreme ways. The results were very striking. On one hand, they earned him an award. On the other, a reprimand from his university. At any rate, he continued to be a productive, and controversial, scholar. At the present time he was (according to the article) deeply engaged in studies of lust.

In one newspaper article, which I found on the web, there was a profile of Hardcastle. He was described as arrogant and pompous, but brilliant; an amazingly inventive researcher, respected but widely disliked by his colleagues. A member of his department, who did not care to be mentioned by name, called him a "bastard." Another quote, from a former research assistant (now at the University of Nebraska), was equally damning: "But you have to give it to the man, he's really got an original way of thinking. Too bad he's such an awful human being."

So this was Ramsey Hardcastle, Lissa's boss. I was curious about the upcoming visit, of course. I hoped he was not engaged in a study of anger and frustration among middle-aged suburban lawyers—I already had quite a few clients who were conducting what Hardcastle might consider a natural experiment along those lines—or lustful thoughts among middle-aged lawyers. It would take waterboarding or the rack to induce me to participate.

At any rate, once we had settled on a time, Hardcastle appeared promptly. He was a tall, impressive-looking man, with distinguished gray hair, a rather haughty face, a hooked Roman nose, and thin lips, which he kept somehow tightly pursed, opening them the minimum required for actual speech. He was immaculately dressed in a suit and tie, and his shoes were coal black and shiny. He looked (to me at least) like a businessman, a CEO, rather than an academic. I would have guessed his age as about 60, plus or minus a few years.

After introducing ourselves to each other, he said, "I'll come straight to the point. I wish to engage your services."

"Which services?" I asked. It was not a question I usually posed to clients and prospective clients. But this man was different. Somehow I doubted that he wanted to talk about his estate plan, some real estate matter, or a claim against someone who had dented his car. His car was surely a Mercedes. A black Mercedes. He had the look of a man who drove a black Mercedes.

"I find myself in an awkward position, and I've been told you're someone who is discreet, and can help me out. And, of course, I understand that anything I say will be treated as confidential."

He paused. I said nothing, waiting for the other shoe to drop. He continued, "What I need is not, in a way, the usual type of help which, uh, an attorney can provide. I have a regular lawyer in San Francisco. His name is Gideon Grambling. He says he knows you."

Indeed, Grambling does know me. I have had dealings with him before; he has slick, upscale offices in San Francisco, and a clientele which is made up, as he would put it, of the "best families, the top people" of San Francisco. "Old money" people. Frankly, our relations had been cool. I doubted that Grambling had anything complimentary to say about me, yet he had induced Hardcastle to make an appointment to see me. "As you well know," he went on, "the sister of my assistant, Miss King, has been murdered."

"Oh yes. Terrible tragedy," I said.

"I have to tell you right now: I never met the woman. Never. The police seem to be totally baffled, which I suppose is standard. Unless they find someone with a smoking gun, they seem to be useless. Complete incompetence. At any rate, I've been told that you're in the process of conducting, shall I say, a discreet investigation of this crime ..."

"Professor Hardcastle," I said, "Let me stop you right there. I don't know what kind of rumors you've heard, or what Gideon has told you, but these rumors are absolutely and categorically false. I am not investigating anything or anybody. That's not my line of work."

"I've heard otherwise," he said, "and I've also heard that you're careful to be, uh, shall we say, sub rosa. I understand that, and it's entirely acceptable to me. I will, of course, pay for your services."

"Professor," I said, trying to be more emphatic, "let me tell you again: you are laboring under a misconception. I'm simply a lawyer, I'm a member of the California Bar, and I specialize in estate work, among other things. And that's it. The only thing I investigate is the Probate Code."

He had a self-satisfied smirk on his face. His eyes darted around the room. My office is neat, orderly, quite respectable, thank you, but nothing compared to the sleek chrome and densely carpeted offices of Gideon Grambling, high above San Francisco, with a staggering view of the Golden Gate Bridge. I had the feeling Hardcastle envisioned me as some sort of Sam Spade character, something out of a film noir with Humphrey Bogart, someone tough and persistent, the type who has sex with a femme fatale in his smoke-filled office just before turning her over to the police to be prosecuted for murder.

"Perhaps I can clarify my, uh, legal needs," he said. "I am separated from my wife, Mildred Hardcastle. She is, frankly, both angry and delusional. She has accused me of having an affair with my assistant, Lissa King. That's completely absurd, but it's the sort of thing she's been saying about me. There are other things, too. Professional misconduct. And now, now that this woman, Geena King, has been found dead, my wife has gotten it into her head that I was sleeping with her too—a woman I never met in my life, whose existence I was barely aware of—and indeed, she has said to more than one person that she believes I am somehow responsible for this woman's death. The situation is, frankly, intolerable. And there's another issue, too. I have been getting, how shall I put it, disturbing letters ..."

"I can understand your feelings," I said. "You're in an unpleasant situation, a difficult situation, and it's natural that you'd like to do something about it. I'm not sure what you *can* do. But whatever it is, it's not something in my line of work. Please believe me; I can't be emphatic enough."

This time, I think I got through to him. He looked disappointed, but I guess he finally accepted that I was not, in fact, Sam Spade, or anything remotely like Sam Spade. I think he finally realized what I was: a suburban lawyer who wrote wills and trusts and helped out clients with their mundane legal needs. I never found out precisely what he thought I could do for him, even if I had been this Sam Spade character. Perhaps he wanted me to solve the murder case. Or to skulk about and figure out what his wife was up to. Or to find out who was sending these disturbing letters.

"Then I take it you decline to act on my behalf?"

"I do. I can't and won't do what you seem to want me to do."

He looked, if not angry, somewhat out of sorts. He got up, obviously to leave my office, when I had a sudden, foolish impulse. I decided to do something that was completely out of line with what I had told him. Out of sheer curiosity, I decided to ask him a question. I wanted to ask him about Geena King's car, the mysterious car—Teddy's new clue.

"One moment, Professor Hardcastle," I said. He turned and looked at me. Not in a friendly way. "Did you know that Miss King's car has turned up?"

"Miss King? My secretary?"

"No, excuse me. The dead woman's car. Did you know about this?"

"Did I know about this? About the woman's car? Why on

earth should I? And why are you asking me questions? Why is this any of your business?"

"Well, it isn't really. But I was, uh, just wondering. I mean, as I told you, I'm not involved, of course, but this dead woman, she was found in my client's house, so naturally, I'm curious about it, just as you are, and my client is terribly upset. And so is your secretary, it's her sister, after all. So it would be a great thing for all of us if we could get to the bottom of this."

"I don't care about the top, middle or bottom. I'm a busy man. I really don't have time to talk about this nonsense. You said you had nothing to do with all this, or were you hiding something from me?"

"No ... no ... I'm sorry. As I said, this woman was found in my client's home. I can't help but be curious."

"Good for you. I'm not the least bit curious."

"Did you know what kind of car this woman had?"

"Good grief, how on earth would I know? My secretary, she has a Chevrolet, I believe, but I don't check on the kind of cars my staff drives. And you have to remember; I never laid eyes on this dead woman. My secretary could have had ten sisters and ten brothers; it would be nothing to me. I don't concern myself with the personal lives of the people who work for me."

He opened the door; but then, apparently, had a slight change of heart. "Now that you mention it—and, I repeat, it's none of your business—but if you are lying, and you're actually connected to some sort of investigation, I don't want you to accuse me of concealing, uh, relevant facts. This car, the dead woman's car, what did it look like?"

"I'm told it was green. A Camry hybrid; bright green."

"I once or twice saw my secretary getting out of a green car in the parking lot. She wasn't driving though. I noticed the color, because it was so ugly. A disgusting shade of green. She told me her car was being serviced, and she had gotten a lift."

"When was this?"

"I don't remember. A while ago. As you can imagine, it didn't loom very large in my life."

"She wasn't driving? Who was?"

"I have no idea. I have the vague impression it was a woman."

"And did that person, whoever it was, come back and pick her up at the end of the day?"

"I have no idea. I don't spy on my people. My secretary left at the regular time. I have no idea how she got home. And now, if you'll excuse me, I have things to do."

Then he left. I was glad he was gone. Good riddance. What an unpleasant man. He had provided me with some information, though. Very likely it was Geena who drove her sister to work when Lissa's car was being serviced. But how Geena's car got where it was, and where it had been in the meantime, remained completely obscure.

I had no desire to see Ramsey Hardcastle ever again. Nor did I. A couple of days later, Professor Ramsey Hardcastle, the Reginald and Fiona Barfuss Professor of Psychology, star of his department at Stanford University, was murdered, strangled to death in his office at about eight or nine o'clock in the evening.

9

Naturally, I had no inkling that any such thing was going to happen, and as soon as Hardcastle was out the door, I dismissed him from my mind.

And yet, what Teddy had told me about the car popping up all of a sudden—that intrigued me, worked on me like an itch that demanded to be scratched. That particular day, I worked somewhat late, and when I had finished redrafting a document I was working on, I realized it was 6:30 in the evening. I should have gone directly home, but instead, I picked up the phone and called Lissa. I imagined she was already home from work.

I know, I know, it was wrong of me. I could hear Celia's voice inside of me, warning me. I could almost hear her saying: "Frank, for God's sake, act rationally for once." But do we ever act rationally? I'm aware that rational action, figuring out pluses and minuses, is the very foundation of economic science, and explains most of life. This was the lesson drummed into our heads by Professor Uglow, who taught Economics 101, one of the most boring classes I ever suffered through. In real life, I wonder, do people behave like that? Are they truly rational?

Sometimes, I suppose. Even me.

I asked Lissa if she knew about the car and told her what Teddy had reported to me. She said, "Oh, God, yes, I know all about it. First of all, Teddy talked to me. And somehow, the police got wind of it. They were swarming all over it ... I guess maybe they got the license number from the motor vehicle department, anyway, they came and hauled it away, looking for fingerprints I suppose, or something else. There was this one policeman, he asked me all sorts of questions, of course, and I didn't know the answers. He did say the keys were in the glove compartment. What I'm wondering is, is Teddy right? He said it wasn't there one day and then the next day, there it was. The police think it was there all the time. They don't know Teddy."

"He's a persistent kid, I'll give him that," I said. "And pretty smart."

"Frank," she said. "If Teddy's right, where was the car before? You know, like I told you, I was running around looking for Geena, mostly in L.A. But I really do think that Geena never left town at all. She drove somewhere, somewhere around here. She met somebody. And that guy, that person, I suppose it was a man, but who knows? Anyway, he killed her and took the body, in the car I guess, and dumped her in that house. Oh God, I can't stand even thinking about it ... and then that person, maybe at night, when nobody was looking, moved the car, probably so nobody would know where it was before. I don't know. I can't figure anything out."

She started crying. I could hear her sobbing on the phone.

"Frank," she said, "who could that be? One guy, from the police department, he wasn't like the rest of them, I think he took pity on me, and he told me a few things. Not that they helped much. He said, they think the body was in the car, but they can't prove it. Whoever did this really cleaned up the car, like it's a professional job. No clue at all, but he must have had her body there, maybe it was wrapped up in something. Frank, this is such a nightmare for me. I can't sleep, I'm depressed. It's bad enough losing my sister. And the arrangements, I told you I had her cremated, and all those horrible details, and nobody to help me. My half-sister, well, we were never close, and she lives too far away. My aunt did come, but somehow it didn't help. And my boss has been awful to me lately, I don't know why. I think he's angry that I took time off, but I felt so desperate when Geena disappeared."

"You did the right thing."

"I have to ask you though. What did my boss want with you? Did he come to see you, like he said he would?"

"Lissa," I said, "the whole thing was embarrassing. He

thought I was investigating your sister's death. I think, among other things, that he wanted to tell me he never met her, didn't know her at all. Is that true, Lissa?"

"I guess it is. As far as I know. But maybe he's lying. Listen, Frank, I have to tell you something. Something I didn't tell you before. When I asked her why she wanted to come up here and live in the Bay Area, she just said, 'I have my reasons.' She asked me what I was doing. I said I was working at Stanford. 'Oh,' she said, 'doing what?' I said, 'The psych department,' I told her, 'I'm some sort of assistant, or secretary, whatever you want to call it.' She said, 'Oh?' She seemed intrigued when I mentioned the psych department. I thought that was funny. I told her I was working for this famous psychologist, Ramsey Hardcastle. And she said: 'Oh my God.' Just like that. 'Oh my God.' And I said, 'Geena, what is it—you know him?' She said, 'Not really.' But I think she was lying. She never mentioned him again. I forgot all about this, it didn't seem important at the time. But now I think ... I don't know what to think."

"You think there was some connection with your boss? What could it be? He was so emphatic with me, said he didn't know her, never met her, never laid eyes on her."

He could have been lying of course. People lie all the time. Even to me. I'm their lawyer, I tell them. I beg them to tell me the truth, but not everybody does.

I thought back to Ramsey's visit. I mean, he *sounded* sincere. But Celia says I'm easily fooled. And it's true. She's much better at smelling lies than I am.

But of course, if Ramsey did know her, if there was some connection, he had a good reason to lie—at least to me. I couldn't see him as a murderer, so it's not as if I suspected him of killing Geena King. I'm sure the last thing he wanted was to get tangled up in this whole miserable affair. Keeping out of it would be worth a lie or two.

"I wish she had confided in me," Lissa said, "told me what was on her mind. Maybe I could have saved her." Her voice broke. I think she was crying again. I said, "Lissa, I'm sorry. I have to go."

I went home in a sour mood.

10

I was surprised, the next day, to find two people waiting for me in the hallway outside my office when I returned from lunch, around 1:30. One was a short, rather dumpy woman, with gray hair tangled around her head. She was, I would guess, around 60. She was bowlegged, and extremely unattractive. She wore a black skirt, a blue blouse, and blue tennis shoes, which somehow didn't seem right for her. She was also wearing dark brown orthopedic stockings. She had puffy cheeks, and small, pig-like eyes.

With her was a young man, extremely skinny, with thin, blondish hair and a very prominent Adam's apple. His eyes, unlike hers, were big and somewhat bulging. He was wearing a rumpled suit, which looked as if he had slept in it, and a garish necktie, knotted very loosely so that his neck, and the Adam's apple, showed clearly.

"Are you waiting for me?" I asked.

"Are you Frank May?" the woman responded, in an annoying, nasal voice.

"Guilty as charged," I said, smiling. She scowled at me. I opened the office door, and they followed me inside.

She said, "I'm Mildred Hardcastle. And this, by the way, is Dr. Philpott Peabody. I believe my husband, Ramsey, came to see you the other day."

"Can I ask why you want to know? Not that there's any secret here."

"Are you his lawyer?"

"I am not."

"I don't believe you," she said. "And you better not lie to me. I'm sick of all these lies. I know he was here. And it wasn't a social call. Ramsey doesn't make social calls. He makes antisocial calls. He's an evil man, a dangerous man, somebody you can't ever trust. Dishonest to the core. I don't think you know how dangerous he can be. I was married to that man, so I know."

Peabody said nothing, but kept nodding his head in agreement. I couldn't help watching the way his Adam's apple bounced up and down.

"Look, Mrs. Hardcastle," I said. "I'm not lying; it's not my style. The plain fact is, I don't represent your husband, I'm not his lawyer, and, yes, it wasn't a social call, but I prefer not to discuss what we talked about. In any event, it had nothing to do with you, and I can't see, honestly, that his visit was any of your business."

"Not my business?" she said, raising her voice. "Not my business? A murder, and it's not my business?"

"What murder are you talking about?"

Her voice became shriller and shriller. "Don't play dumb! I'll go to the bar association, if necessary, and I'll tell them about you! You have no business helping him. The man should be arrested, put away for life. First he has an affair with his secretary, and then, as if that wasn't shameful enough, he goes after her sister. And now she's dead! He killed her, I tell you. Probably to shut her up."

She was pounding on the desk. Her friend, Philpott, sat rigidly in his chair, staring straight forward. Mildred seemed seriously deranged to me, and who knows what Philpott was like? At least he was quiet. I had this overwhelming desire (naturally) to get rid of them, to get them out of the office. I tried to act calmly. "That's a serious accusation," I said. "I mean, why do you say that? According to your husband, he didn't even know the woman, had never met her, actually."

"Oho!" she said, in a loud, triumphal tone, "So you admit you talked about the murder. You're not even a good liar, Mr. Lawyer."

That did it. I said, "I think you'd better leave." I tried to make my voice sound extremely authoritative, which isn't easy for me. She did leave, eventually, but not, I think, because of me. First, she railed on about intellectual fraud, about how Ramsey Hardcastle had cheated the National Science Foundation, how his work was a tissue of lies—and immoral to boot—how he dominated his department, and ruined everybody's life. Philpott kept nodding in agreement. But then, without waiting for a response, she got up and left. She had said her piece. She stormed out of the office with Philpott Peabody trailing behind her. As she left I heard her shouting something; exactly what, I couldn't quite make out. I hoped that nobody would hear her, although she was extremely loud. It was embarrassing. Unfortunately, at that very moment, one of the other tenants of the building (an orthodontist) came up the stairs and witnessed this ridiculous scene.

This is not something that happens to your typical orthodontist, I suppose.

When she was gone, I breathed a sigh of relief, and reminded myself how wise my dear wife is, always telling me to mind my own business and avoid these miserable affairs. "Celia," I said, as if she was in the room, "I'll have nothing to do with it. I swear."

It was a promise I could not keep, especially because, as I said before, Ramsey Hardcastle was murdered that very night.

11

I read the news in the *San Francisco Chronicle*. It was on the front page: "Stanford Professor Murdered in his Office." Indeed, it was national news as well. I learned that the story was reported in the *New York Times*, and I suppose all the other newspapers that cull stories from the *New York Times*. The death of Ramsey Hardcastle was worth national mention. He was an important and imposing figure in the academic world.

The subtitle in the *Chronicle* story named the victim. The minute I saw Hardcastle's name, I had an awful feeling in the pit of my stomach. I read the rest of the story in a kind of intense panic. The professor had been alone in his office. He had come back after eating dinner at home, apparently by himself. The crime took place sometime between eight and nine. The psychology building was largely deserted, and it was rare for the professor (the story said) to work that late in his office. There had been obviously some sort of struggle. The place was ransacked, with papers strewn all over the floor, file drawers open and chairs overturned. Hardcastle had been beaten, perhaps during the struggle, and then strangled with "what appeared to be a scarf of some sort." The police, according to the story, "were following up a number of leads." Then there were various quotes from people in the field of psychology, about his work, how much he had contributed to the discipline, statements from the chair of the department (Dr. Maud Edelweiss), and from the President of the American Psychological Association.

There was also a paragraph, in rather poor taste, I felt, which reported that the professor "had not been popular with many of his colleagues, or with his graduate students" and a quote from one student, unidentified, who said, "I'm sorry he's dead, I wouldn't want anybody to die, not even Hitler. But to tell the truth, Hardcastle was an absolute bastard, and arrogant to boot. Nobody liked him. He had a mean streak a mile wide. That's why he was an expert on anger and cruelty. It takes one to know one."

A side story helped explain this comment; it described the famous studies of cruelty and anger in children, and the boiling controversy over those studies, and included a quote from a member of the Stanford faculty to the effect that such studies "would be completely taboo today, and one wonders how they were ever approved in the first place." That was just what I had wondered when I'd googled him.

Another psychology professor (also anonymous) said, "you had to wonder about his own children, I mean, did he torture them too?" The article explained that Dr. Hardcastle had been married four times, and was separated from his latest wife, Mildred. He had three children, two sons and a daughter, who were the product of earlier marriages. He also had two grand-children. Alexander Hardcastle, his older son, lived, in what was described as a commune, just outside of Eugene, Oregon, and spent his days making candles; Hardcastle's daughter, Susannah, was married to a dentist in Wichita, Kansas; the second son, Jason, lived in New Zealand, and was a "film-maker and director." The family, according to the article "was not close."

"Celia," I said, "did you see this story?" I showed it to her. She said, "Don't tell me he was a client, Frank."

"No, not a client. But this guy did come to see me, just the other day."

She made some comments—perfectly justified, I have to admit—about the strange, demonic fate that seemed to pursue my clients, and how often they ended up dead. "A person might think you killed them yourself."

"Darling, I told you: He wasn't a client," I said, rather feebly.

"Whatever. He came to visit you, didn't he? Now he's dead. I should send Harlow Gooch to your office. Maybe *he'd* end up dead. I wish." Gooch was an assistant principal at Celia's school, a fussy and bureaucratic man who got on her nerves almost on a daily basis.

Despite Harlow Gooch, Celia seemed to be in an excellent mood that evening; even the death of a non-client who had just come to see me was not enough to ruin it. "There's a new woman P.E. teacher, you know, in physical education. She's not married; actually, she's divorced, and she seems quite nice, I'd say she's about 35. I was wondering if she might be just the one for Adam." Adam, of course, was Adam Finkel, the math teacher with the terrible complexion. As I think I said, it was Celia's goal in life to get him married or at least in some sort of relationship. This new woman appearing on the scene was enough to get Celia excited. "I'm sure she'd like to get married again, or at least find a partner. I think she'd like Adam, I really do, once she gets to know him."

Hope springs eternal. I was skeptical that a physical education teacher, presumably very fit and athletic, and perhaps good-looking, would have any interest in Adam, whose shyness was legendary, and whose face would stop the proverbial clock; not to mention that he lived with an aged and cranky mother on the verge of dementia. But I held my tongue. Perhaps Celia knew something about the situation that escaped me. Or was it simply her faith that, once a person got to know Adam, got to plumb the depths of his soul, they could and would look past the shyness and the terrible complexion. To me it seemed unlikely.

"About this Hardcastle person," Celia said. "I'm worried, Frank. Could you be a possible suspect? Do the police know the professor came to see you?"

"I hope not," I said.

The very thought of a visit from the police sent chills up and down my spine. I fled to the family room, and turned on the television set. I needed a distraction.

The public television station had a feature about leaf-cutting ants. Amazing little tropical creatures. They don't actually eat the leaves; they cut them, drag them to their nest, make a sort of mulch out of them, grow fungus on the mulch, and then they proceed to eat the fungus. Why they prefer fungus to nice juicy leaves was never explained. There are, it seems, billions of these ants. None of them, fortunately, in my backyard. Each nest contains millions of these tiny insects, all of them (the program said) sterile females. What happened to the males? Gone, apparently. The photographs of these sly little things, munching on fungus deep under the soil, struck me as absolutely amazing. It makes you wonder how it was possible to get a camera down there—or were those photos taken in a lab or something?

That mystery was never solved, at least not on the program. One thing though, these fascinating ants drove Ramsey Hardcastle right out of my mind. Ramsey Hardcastle and apparently everything else—because I realized later that I had fallen fast asleep in front of our new flat-screen television set. The ant program was long gone, replaced by a documentary on stately homes somewhere on the Balkan Peninsula.

* * *

I had a good night's sleep, which is always therapeutic. I got to the office at 9, saw two clients, worked on some documents, and was thinking about lunch when I got a very agitated phone call from Margot.

"Frank," she said, "do you have time? I simply have to come see you."

"What's this about, Margot?"

"It's this latest thing, Frank. This professor. The one who got murdered. I just have to talk to somebody about this; it's driving me crazy! I can be at your place in, oh, half an hour."

I should have asked her what exactly was driving her crazy, but I thought better of it. And, though it might have been a bit callous of me, I told her to come after lunch. I had sushi in mind, and I wasn't going to be deprived of it by a mere client.

She showed up at two, a bit out of breath. "I took time off from work," she said. "I couldn't concentrate anyway, I've been absolutely useless. I told them I had a toothache and needed to see the dentist. I don't like lying, Frank, but I couldn't say, 'I'm going to see my lawyer.'"

She began crying at that point, and I handed her a tissue from the box I keep on my desk. It gets surprisingly frequent use.

"Frank, I don't know why this is happening to us. First that woman, and now this professor. The police keep asking us questions, me and Jim. Of course, I know absolutely nothing whatsoever about this man. I never met him in my life. But of course they don't believe me. Don't you work at Stanford? Well, I do. So does Jim. Are you sure you never had any contact with the professor? I swore I hadn't. Jim had to admit he was at some sort of staff meeting, something about pensions, and this professor was there. But so were dozens of other people, and the provost of the University. Honestly, I had to wonder, did they actually think we killed this man? They know we didn't kill that woman, we weren't even here at the time; but still, I mean, they're so suspicious. I don't really blame them. Somebody put a dead body in our house, and then they find out she's got a sister who works for this professor at Stanford, and now the professor is dead too, and so they're back asking questions. It's like torture, and then I get all agitated, and they think, oho, she's hiding something. I feel like I'm going to have a breakdown, I really do. Jim, I know he's upset, too, but he's trying to help me, and somebody has to act normally. Maybe I'm extra sensitive because I'm pregnant. I'm nauseated anyway, and I have trouble sleeping."

"I know it's hard," I said, for want of anything better.

"I told them over and over again, I never had any contact with Ramsey Hardcastle, why would I know him? Neither of us went to Stanford, Jim went to UC Santa Barbara, and, like I told you, he had no contact with the guy, not really. The whole thing is so crazy!"

I handed her another tissue and told her, in as sincere a voice as I could muster, that I felt her pain, and realized it was an awful situation, but what did she think I could do about it? Of course I knew the answer already: solve the case. Find out who killed Geena King; find out who killed Ramsey Hardcastle. "I would if I could, Margot," I said.

"Oh, Frank, you've got to. Don't you have contacts? The police department, you must know somebody because of your clients ..."

I tried to explain to her, as patiently as I could, that I had no such contacts—my clients came to me with estate problems, divorce problems, real estate problems, all sorts of problems— but nothing that involved crime, murder, or the police. That was mostly true, although I did have a client, the widow of a real estate broker, a woman in her 60's, who was foolish enough to go on one of these online dating sites, and who ended up marrying a young psychopath half her age. The marriage was a disaster, and she eventually came to me crying and asking me to do something, anything, and for help getting a restraining order.

Restraining orders are not my normal line of business, and fortunately, before anything more happened, she decided to drop the restraining order, and simply leave the area. She had a sister in Vancouver, so she packed up and left. At any rate, it was no longer my problem. If it was anybody's problem, that headache would plague some lawyer in British Columbia. Of course, I lost her as a client, but it was just as well.

"Frank, I was so hoping you could help me," Margot said, dabbing her eyes with the tissue. "This whole business with the professor, it brings up all the old stuff again. I mean, maybe they think we hired somebody to kill that woman, though why would we do such a thing, and why would we have the killer bring the body to our house? And now, they want to know what we have to do with Tina Gilchrist ..."

"Tina Gilchrist? Teddy's mother?"

"Yes. Because Teddy had the key. And they seem to think there's some connection with his mother. I mean, a connection to this professor. We don't know Tina very well, I mean, she seems very nice, and Teddy is a fine boy; they're sort of neighbors, but this isn't a very neighborly neighborhood and people keep to themselves. Still, we did hire Teddy, and we've used him before, and they think the whole thing is suspicious, Teddy's key and all that. And besides, this dead woman was Lissa King's sister, and she was living in Lissa King's house, so supposedly we could have known her. But we didn't. Not really. Lissa King, maybe I met her once, when she was collecting for the Cancer Fund and came to the house, but Tina Gilchrist knew her better, and so their dirty little minds think there's something all of us are hiding, who knows, maybe a conspiracy of some sort. The whole thing is so awful."

She calmed down after a while, and I told her the affair would maybe blow over. The police were very good, very efficient—in this area anyway—and so, I told her, somebody would be arrested shortly, at least this was likely to happen, it usually does. Three tissues later, she was ready to go home, and I heaved a sigh of relief.

I did wonder a bit about Tina Gilchrist. After all, Tina could have gotten hold of the key to Margot's house—if anybody could. And I couldn't help asking myself why the police would have any interest in her in connection with the late Ramsey Hardcastle.

Maybe they were having an affair. Not that any such thing seemed particularly likely. He was a world-famous professor. She was a suburban housewife. But people do strange things.

I sat back in my chair, and let my mind wander. Ramsey and Tina. Lovers. An odd couple, of course, and maybe that's why they're not getting along. Ramsey Hardcastle is not easy to get along with; everybody says that. And, in the end, he decides he's tired of her. She comes to his office to plead with him. They have a furious argument. She kills him.

Poor Teddy. What would happen to him if his mother was arrested for murder?

12

This was my week to be confronted with women who were extremely upset, and who somehow thought I could be of some service. Margot's visit was followed by a one from Lissa King, who called me in a state of panic, which she refused to discuss on the phone. "They listen in, don't they?" she said.

"Lissa, I don't think anybody is listening in, I really don't."

But she was adamant; she had to see me in person. I put her off for a day. I had no particular desire to talk to her. But there she was, the very next day, sitting across from me, white as a sheet. I tried to avoid looking at her chest, which was heaving with sorrowful emotion.

Basically, she recited the same litany as Margot: "I can't sleep, I can't eat, I'm in a total panic, Frank. You have to help me."

"Is it ... about your sister? And now your boss?"

"They think I killed him, Frank. They think I killed my boss. I'm terrified. I don't want to go to jail."

"They think you killed him? Where did they get that idea from?"

"He was strangled. With a scarf. Did you know that? Well, he was. And ... the worst of it is, it was my scarf, and they know it!"

"My God, Lissa. You were there?"

"Yes, I was there. I mean, no, I wasn't there when ... when this thing happened. I was there earlier. I must have left my

76

scarf in his office. But he wasn't dead when I was there—I swear it. I don't know anything about this awful thing."

"Well, then you have nothing to worry about," I said. "You were his secretary, you worked for him, you forgot your scarf in his office, and, well, somebody came by and killed him, and used the darn thing. That's all. You went home at five o'clock, you forgot all about the scarf."

She hesitated. "But it wasn't five o'clock. When I said I was there, I didn't mean just during the day. Yes, I went home at five o'clock. But I came back ... around eight. I came to his office. And, on the way out, I saw that awful woman, Mildred, his ex-wife—I think they're divorced; maybe they're just separated—and she's an absolute dragon lady! She grabbed hold of me and said terrible things, I won't even repeat them, they were so vile; and she was with Philpott Peabody, and he knows me of course, he was in the department, so I can't deny that I was there. This is such a nightmare, first my sister, now this. I'm going out of my mind, I really am."

"Lissa, I'm terribly sorry. But surely they don't think it was you, even though you went to the office. Why should you do anything to him? It doesn't make sense. But, Lissa, can I ask you something: what *were* you doing there? I don't mean to pry, but ..."

"He called me and said I had to come, it was very important. I said, 'Professor, it's night time, I really don't want to come to the campus, it's late, it's dark outside.' But he insisted. Said he'd make it up to me. And when I came there, of course, the building was locked, but I have a key. Anyway, I went up to his office and he seemed very agitated. He said he was going to 'clean up his office,' that's what he said, 'clean up his office,' get rid of stuff. And I said, 'Now? It's eight o'clock, can't it wait until tomorrow? Why is this such a crisis?' I mean, I was really annoyed. He was always rude, thoughtless, and bossy. But this was over the top.

"Of course, he paid no attention to what I said. He went right on talking. He said he was working on his old files and he wanted me to take certain documents and get rid of them. I tell you, I was really angry, so I just refused, and left. I guess I was so upset and angry that I forgot my scarf. And of course, my fingerprints are all over the place. I said to the cops, 'Of course they are! I was the man's secretary, I was in and out of his office all the time.'"

Somehow, I had the feeling she was not telling me the truth. Not the whole truth, anyway. I can't say why I felt that way—something in her tone of voice maybe. "Lissa," I said, "really, I feel for you. You have to understand though; I can't do anything for you. I could recommend someone ..."

She made no response. Instead, she burst into tears. I handed her another tissue. At this rate, I would have to buy another box. I felt helpless. Celia never cries. She's made of sterner stuff. When we go to a sad movie, I'm the one that ends up blubbering. For want of anything better to say, I asked Lissa if she had any idea who might have done this thing—who might be responsible?

"Oh, Frank," she said, "lots of people could have done this. He was such an awful man. I think everybody hated him. The other professors, especially the younger ones. He was so bossy! Always insisted on getting his way. And the staff, no one could stand him! He was such a big shot, world famous, you know, he had four honorary degrees, including one from someplace in Switzerland, I can't remember the name, or was it Sweden? He never let you forget how important he was. And he was an absolute terror to anyone he supervised."

"Anybody in particular? Somebody who might have, uh, hated him enough to kill him? I mean, you were working there."

"Well, just about everybody hated him. But if I had to single somebody out, it would be Professor Peabody. Philpott Peabody. He had been there a few years, and he was up for tenure—and I think he expected it, he had a lot of publications and research grants—but Dr. Hardcastle made sure he didn't get the promotion. I think it was just spite on his part. I heard that Hardcastle insisted the work was no good. I don't go to faculty meetings, I just hear things, rumors, but it must be true. He wasn't renewed or whatever you call it, and he has to look

for another job. And, well, there's all the gossip about Peabody."

"Gossip?"

"About him and Mildred Hardcastle. Can you imagine?
He's a good thirty years younger than she is. And she's ugly too.
She hated her husband like poison. I can't believe there's
anything, well, physical, between Mildred and Peabody, you
just have to take a look at them. But they're thick as thieves.
They've been making complaints to the government, that's
what I heard."

"Complaints? To the government? What sort of complaints?"

"That Dr. Hardcastle was mismanaging research funds.
Something like that. Oh, Frank, maybe they're the ones that
killed him. They were there that night, I told you that; I saw
them hanging around the building."

"Well, Lissa," I said, "I'm sure the police know about all of
this, maybe they'll arrest them, you just wait and see." Of
course, I had no idea whether this was true or not. I just said it.
My point was that this was a matter for the police, and only the
police. They had the manpower, crime labs, and all that
forensic skill. I wanted her to lean on them—not me.

And of course this *was* a police matter. Still, my sunny
optimism and my assurances that the police would no doubt
crack the case wide open, and very soon: all this was construct-
ed out of thin air. In fact, I had no idea where the case stood or
what the police were doing.

And Lissa herself, was she a suspect? I doubted it. I
couldn't see her as a killer. Of course, I did have the feeling she
was lying about something. And her story about the scarf—to
me, it didn't quite ring true.

I was happy to talk to people (despite Celia's warnings),
and happy to lean back in my chair and try to figure things out
(so far with no apparent success). But a more active role? No
thanks. I wanted, particularly, nothing to do with Mildred
Hardcastle.

That was easier said than done.

13

I said I wanted nothing to do with Mildred Hardcastle, but she, it turns out, did not reciprocate. I began getting emails from her, demanding that I turn over to her any "papers, records, or documents provided to me by the late Dr. Ramsey Hardcastle." I responded, of course, that I had no such papers. The emails were followed by a phone call from Sylvan Platt. He told me, over the phone, that he was handling the estate of Ramsey Hardcastle.

"Congratulations," I said.

"Are you being sarcastic? Do you know the family?"

"Well," I said, "I actually met Dr. Hardcastle once, and I've met his wife. Or ex-wife, I'm not sure which she is."

"They weren't divorced," he said. "That was on the horizon and they were consulting lawyers—not me, by the way, I don't do divorces. I wish to god they had gotten divorced before he died. It would make things that much simpler. Anyway, I need to talk to you."

"What about?"

"Well, the estate. Can we do lunch tomorrow?" Lunch was important to Sylvan—and to me, too, but not to the same degree. Sylvan was currently single, and I don't think his evening meals, if he was home alone, were up to his standards. Hence his passion for lunch.

"A lot of restaurants," he told me once, "do a better lunch than dinner. You wouldn't think so, but it's true. Take that Chinese restaurant in San Carlos, the one with the word 'dragon' in its name. I had a marvelous buffet lunch there, but at night, it's mediocre. Maybe a different chef."

This time, Sylvan suggested Japanese food, and we agreed to meet at an upscale restaurant in Palo Alto, Sushi Delight. I arrived on time; Sylvan was late. I had never been to the place before. It was a big restaurant, with a sushi bar on one end and regular tables in a large room. I noticed a couple of side rooms, set up so people could squat Japanese style when they ate. I tried this once, at a Japanese restaurant in San Francisco—it was utter torture.

An attractive young woman in a kimono led me to a table, divided off from other tables with bamboo poles. Then Sylvan appeared.

We shook hands, and he sat down.

"Let's order first," Sylvan said. He was obviously a great aficionado of Japanese food, along with other cuisines, of course. He ordered sashimi, and then individual examples of the most exotic sushi on the menu, raw shrimp, sea urchin, and other delicacies, which he asked for using their Japanese names, pronouncing them with great enthusiasm. My own choice would have been tempura, but I felt cowed by Sylvan's behavior, so I ordered some sort of noodle dish that seemed harmless to me. I do like sushi, but I'm too frightened to wander far from what you might call Beginner's Sushi, or Sushi 101, that is, cucumber rolls and California rolls and other dishes that Sylvan no doubt sneered at. He was, I have to admit, too polite, or perhaps too absorbed in his eating, to criticize my choices of food.

Sylvan, when the food came, handled the chopsticks as if he had been born to it. He ate with great enthusiasm. Then he put down his chopsticks, looked me in the eye, and began talking. "Life is full of twists and turns, you know? Full of surprises. Like what happened to Ramsey Hardcastle. I understand you knew him."

"Knew him is a bit of an exaggeration. I met him once." I should have added: once was enough.

"Well, I did know him. I was his lawyer. Handled his af-fairs, we had these estate planning sessions, I made out a will, an advanced health care directive, a living trust—you know the drill, Frank. He consulted me, too, about his divorce, or, I should say, his proposed divorce. I don't do divorces, but I recommended Jennifer Forest, she's the best in the business, and as tough as nails. But, unfortunately, he died before he could, uh, get rid of his wife. Unfortunate for me, too. I have to deal with that woman, do you know her? An absolute mental case. Vicious, irrational. Driving me crazy. Honestly, despite the fact that it's a big estate, well, fairly big, and ordinarily, I'd be pleased as punch to have it, I'm sorely tempted to give it up."

Was he going to suggest giving it to *me*? Surely not. Didn't Ramsey Hardcastle have children? They would make the decision, I suppose, if Sylvan bowed out.

"It's that woman I wanted to talk to you about," Sylvan continued.

"Oh?"

"Because of your involvement," he said, lowering his voice.

"My involvement?"

"It's an awkward situation. My client was murdered. That's a first for me and the absolute last, if I have anything to say about it. You, on the other hand ... you've had, uh, clients who ... you know what I mean. And everybody's talking about your, uh, skills in these matters."

"Really, Sylvan ..."

"No, no, don't say anything. Let me finish. This awful woman, Mildred, she was totally out of control. She accused him of everything under the sun, including murder. Said he killed his secretary's sister and dumped her body in a house belonging to your client. According to her, Ramsey was sleeping with both of these women. They had threesomes or whatever. The woman, as I said, is a mental case. It all sounds weird to me. Unlikely, anyway. So now, she's got the idea that this secretary, Lissa King, killed Ramsey. Revenge she says, revenge for her sister, and she's raising a huge stink about it, along with claims of fraud on the government, and, for all I know, she'll end up accusing him of assassinating Martin Luther King Jr. and President Kennedy, or, for that matter,

Abraham Lincoln. Meanwhile, somebody turned around and assassinated him! I tell you, the woman is completely insane."

"OK Sylvan," I said, "but what on earth does that have to do with me? Yes, Margot Williams is a client, and ... yes, it was her house where this, uh, body was dumped. Lissa's sister. Still, I don't see the connection ..."

"But you have to admit, there *is* a connection. It's not two random murders, don't you agree? And since you're investigating the first one ..."

"Sylvan, stop right there," I said. "I'm investigating nothing. Nothing. Period. End of statement."

"Aren't you trying to protect your client's interests? There was a murder in her house. That makes her a suspect."

"Sylvan," I said, "you're watching too much TV. First of all, no, I don't think Margot Williams is a suspect. She was a hundred miles away when this woman was killed. And second, no, I'm not doing anything about the case, why should I? That's a job for the police."

He looked at me, with his chopsticks poised in the air. "So ... you would not be interested, am I right, in, uh, certain information ..."

"Information?"

"I heard, through the grapevine, that you were 'on the case,' as they say ... No, no, don't deny it. Hear me out. I happen to have some inside information."

Of course the idea of inside information intrigued me. On the other hand, I had to convince him that I was not "on the case," that I was not some sort of suburban version of Hercule Poirot or Perry Mason or Sam Spade or whatever, and that I had no role in this matter, and, if I were so foolish as to try to play a role, my dear wife would be extremely angry. I'm not sure Sylvan was convinced, in fact I'm sure he was not; but he did say, "Well, whatever. I have to talk to somebody about this. Just hear me out."

I had to agree. And, frankly, I wanted to hear what he had to say.

"Ramsey came to see me," Sylvan said, "a couple of days before somebody did him in. He said he was very troubled. Said that there were disturbing things going on. I asked him, what he meant. He said he was getting 'threats.' I said, 'Threats? What kind of threats?' He said, 'Well, threats, you know what that means, threats of violence.' I immediately thought about Mildred, I mean, the woman is unbalanced, she hates him, and she's capable of anything. I said, 'You mean Mildred.' He said, 'Well, yes, there's Mildred. But not just Mildred. Somebody else.' I asked him, 'Who?' And he said, 'Would you believe me if I said, I'm not sure? Or suppose I just didn't want to say, could we leave it at that?' And I said, 'Well, whatever.' And then he said, 'The question is, is there any way for me to protect myself?'"

"Wow."

"I said, it wasn't my department, but I suppose not hearing a name, well, that made it difficult for anybody else to do something, though maybe the police, they could look into this. I asked him, 'How are you getting these threats? Is it email, or letters, or phone calls, or what?' He didn't answer, and I guess he decided I was pretty useless on this matter, which of course I am, and I didn't get anything much out of him. He was acting very peculiar, I must say. I suggested he might want to hire a private detective, and he said, 'Maybe.' Oh, and then he said something even stranger. He asked me if I liked chamber music."

"Chamber music?"

"You know, quartets, classical quartets, Mozart, Beethoven."

"I said, 'You know, Ramsey, I do. I go regularly to the concerts, at the Bing Auditorium, in Stanford. Brand new auditorium. I don't like the acoustics, but they get some terrific musicians. Why do you ask? Are you a music lover?' He said, 'No,' and he asked if I happened to go to a concert, and then he mentioned the name, but I must say I can't remember it and—I guess I hadn't gone to it—I couldn't remember why.

"Then it came to me, I remembered why I didn't go; it was because this quartet was made up of four Hungarians, and they had a thing for avant-garde music. They would do some Mozart quartet, say, but then they would also play one of those modern, God-awful things, no melody at all, and the music sounds like four alley cats screaming. I never go to those. I mean, Frank, would you believe it, I read about one piece where there was a goldfish bowl with lines drawn on it, like a music clef, you know what I mean? And goldfish were swimming around, and the four players stood around the goldfish bowl and played notes that I suppose corresponded to the way the goldfish were swimming. Can you imagine?

"Well, I'm rambling, Frank. This quartet, the one Ramsey mentioned, the Hungarian one, I definitely didn't go. I mean, what's with Hungarians? I love the soup; have you ever had cold cherry soup? But the people—well, I shouldn't generalize, but I had a Hungarian client once, he was completely mad. Said he was married to a cousin of Zsa Zsa Gabor. Anyway, I asked Ramsey why he was so interested in this quartet, and he said, 'Never mind.' He had obviously decided not to tell me anything more, and he clammed up completely. But honestly, Frank, from the tone, and the context, I imagine it must have had something to do with these threats. Maybe he was murdered by a Hungarian quartet. All of them together."

"Don't be ridiculous," I said. "Somebody strangled him. I don't think that's a group project."

"Well, maybe the cello guy strangled him, and the two violinists held his arms, and the viola player did something else. Who knows? Anyway, all this stuff about Hungarian musicians, it could be important, Frank. Don't you think so?"

"I guess I do. Did you tell your story to the police?"

"Oh, absolutely. Well, not exactly ... I talked about the threats. To be honest, I didn't mention the Hungarian quartet. It seemed too ... flaky. And about the threats, they listened, they seemed to be really interested, but since I couldn't give them a name, or anything else, there's really nothing to go on. I suppose, if they found threatening letters, among his papers, but naturally they wouldn't tell me if they did. And Frank, there's something else."

"Oh? Like what?"

"He started talking about the dead woman, you know, the one in your client's house. I said, oh, wasn't that terrible, blah

blah, she was your secretary's sister, wasn't she? And he said, 'Yes she was.' I asked, 'Did you know her?' And he paused, you know, didn't say anything for a second or two, and then he said, 'Actually, no, I didn't know her. And I couldn't care less, if my stupid secretary's stupid sister goes and gets herself killed.' I thought, what a sweetheart he is, no empathy whatsoever. But then he said, 'I resent being dragged into it, it's not my fault.' I said, 'Of course it isn't your fault, why would you think so?' But I was wondering, hey, what is this? What did he mean, 'dragged into it'? I repeated what I said, like, 'Ramsey, why would anybody think it was your fault?' He just scowled and didn't say another word. And that was that. Do you by any chance know what he was talking about, Frank?"

"No, not a clue. Look: I met the man exactly once. He came to see me, God knows why. I guess he thought I was investigating, or something. Anyway, when he saw me, he told me he never met the woman, and didn't know anything about her. Weird. Maybe he was lying."

"People do that sort of thing," Sylvan said. "Lying, I mean. I lie all the time, to clients. It's completely necessary. And they lie right back. It's part of the game. By the way, Frank, do you want dessert?"

I always want dessert, but I said, "Only if you do, Sylvan."

He said, "Not here, though. Asian cultures have no concept of dessert. It's a serious flaw. I love Asian food, all of it, Chinese, Thai, Vietnamese, Japanese, everything. But dessert, no thank you. I know a place two blocks from here where they have artisanal ice cream. Marvelous stuff. I know the guys who own it. I did some law work for them, once. They're a bit weird, but they make fabulous ice cream, they've got a little shop in San Francisco, this one down here is a branch. They claim their ice cream is different; it has a spiritual quality. Myself, I think it's the high butterfat content. Or maybe the high price. Costs twice as much as regular ice cream."

"I'm game," I said.

"I do think they have a point, you know, about spiritual food. Food can be spiritual. Things we take into our bodies, you know what I mean? Like people say, you are what you eat. Now, take sushi, for example. It's sort of pure, sort of absolute, I mean, especially the raw fish and the seaweed. I can't explain it. I suppose you can make anything spiritual, I mean, anything you eat. It's a question of attitude, maybe. You know, there could even be such a thing as a spiritual cheeseburger. Harder to do, though. Anyway, let's go for the spiritual ice cream."

We went. The shop was called Frozen in Time. I had two scoops of chocolate, made (they said) from rare Ghanaian cocoa beans. I found it rather disappointing. Lacking in spirituality, I suppose. And it was, as promised, fearfully expensive. Maybe the price was the spiritual part. Sylvan, on the other hand, had some other concoction, I forget what exactly, and told me it was marvelous.

As I walked back to my car, I kept thinking about the things Sylvan told me. Somebody was threatening Ramsey. Maybe more than one person. And he was genuinely frightened. For good reason, as it turned out. And what was the connection between Ramsey and Geena King? *Was* there a connection? Did I dare ask Lissa? And had Ramsey lied to me? That wouldn't be a first. And what, if anything, did a Hungarian quartet have to do with Ramsey's death?

Lissa. She had definitely lied to me. There was something decidedly fishy about her story: Did Ramsey really call her up and insist that she come to his office in the evening? Why was she there? Of course I had no way of knowing. It just didn't seem quite rational to me. But, as I said, for most of us, rationality's basically not our thing.

According to Lissa, Ramsey wanted her to take some documents. She said she refused. What was so important about these documents that he had to get rid of them, and that very night? Or was I missing the point? And now Mildred was demanding that I turn over any papers or documents I had received from Ramsey Hardcastle. Of course I had no such papers. Was she talking about the papers Ramsey had been trying to get rid of? What sort of papers would a professor of psychology have in his office that suddenly turned out to be so ... well, fateful?

Eventually, I would get answers. I would even find out more about the Hungarian quartet. But for the moment I was completely in the dark.

14

I thought I was through with Mildred Hardcastle, and a good thing, too. But I was wrong. She turned up at my office, unexpectedly, bursting on the scene with an angry, red-flushed face, dragging Philpott along with her. She plumped herself down on a chair, breathing heavily. Philpott explained the situation: "She climbed the stairs instead of taking the elevator. She doesn't trust elevators because she had a bad experience once."

I'm on the second floor of a three-story building. This time, and this time only, I wished I was a San Francisco lawyer with an office like Gideon Grambling's. His place is high up in a very tall building, on something like the 20th floor. His huge windows offer people a stunning view. Gideon is immune from Mildred Hardcastle. She could not possibly climb all those stairs.

The woman was actually gasping for breath now, and I wondered if she was having some kind of attack. Philpott did not seem worried. She recovered herself, and began to harangue me about her husband.

"Corruption, corruption, corruption!" she said. "The whole society is corrupt. The system is rigged! Science?! There is no science anymore, it's all politics. I know. I was married to the man. He was rotten to the core."

"Mrs. Hardcastle," I began, "I really don't see ..."

"Nobody sees," she says. "Nobody sees, nobody hears, nobody thinks. See no evil, etc. The public is a great beast. A beast. A herd of ignorant sheep," and she began braying and making animal noises, no doubt to illustrate this profound point. Philpott gave her a look of utter devotion, and patted her hand gently with his.

"I warn you," she said, "if you touch pitch, you get defiled yourself. This man was corrupt. All his dealings were corrupt. Do you want to know about all those government grants he got? The millions they gave him, the National Institutes of Science, or whatever they're called. He twisted them around his fingers. He had his cronies there, in Washington. Believe me, when it all comes out, there'll be hell to pay."

The mystery to me was why she ever married this man who she despised so deeply. Or, more to the point, why Ramsey Hardcastle had ever married this woman. To me, it seemed utterly incomprehensible. She was ugly, shrill, and a borderline mental case. And he was ... well, he was what he was. Whatever attracted him to her? Was she different when he married her? I can't imagine that she was ever the kind of woman who could catch his fancy.

But so many marriages seem utterly incomprehensible. I have clients, married clients, divorced clients, separated clients, cohabiting couples, same-sex couples, couples in all shapes and sizes, and very often I look at a couple, and I ask myself, "How in God's name did they ever get together, and why? And what happened later?" There was, for so many of them, no such thing as living happily ever after. Was there some magical event that transformed Ramsey, say, from a prince into a frog? Or turned her into a fat old crone, a witch on a broomstick? When did the milk start to curdle, and the cheese begin to rot? Or: How could he (or she) have ever made such a full-blown catastrophic mistake?

For that matter, here was another odd couple sitting right in front of me. Mildred and Philpott were certainly an unusual pair. She was a harridan in her 60's, with stringy gray hair, seriously overweight, and so bow-legged that she almost seemed oval-shaped. He was a man in his 30's, skinny as a rail, with a major nose problem, receding chin, balding spot in the center of his skull, and that protruding Adam's apple. Were they having an affair? Actual sex? It seemed improbable. Yet as she talked, he seemed to hang on her every word, like a devoted lover—or perhaps more like the disciple of a guru.

She was going on and on about corruption, how dishonest everybody was at the science institutes in Washington that handed out money to her husband. She kept repeating herself, over and over, the same litany of complaints. It was never clear to me if she was accusing him of bribery, or just some rotten form of cronyism. Then she ranted and raved about all his misdeeds in the department, and how that, too, was a form of corruption. "And what he did to Phil here! Disgraceful."

I tried, as gently as I could, to let them know that whatever they might think, I had nothing to do with this affair. I might as well have been talking to two stones. She clearly thought I was deeply, passionately involved.

"In case you're interested, Mr. Lawyer," she said, "we know who killed him." That caught my attention.

"You do?"

"That woman killed him," Mildred said. "The slut who works for him. Lissa King. He deserved it, oh, yes, he deserved it, and she's the one who did it. You're playing with fire when you get involved with that kind of woman. There's a price to be paid for her body. It's a form of prostitution. But she paid him back. You know, the building is locked at night—the building where he was killed—you need a key to get in. We were there. We saw her. She had a key, remember that."

Lissa had told me that already: that she saw them that night outside the building. I said, "Can I ask you, what *you* were doing there?" I was surprised at my own courage in asking this question.

"None of your business! We never went in. She did, though. Maybe there were doing some kind of sexual thing, and she strangled him. It's perfectly clear. The police are too stupid to see something right in front of their noses."

I couldn't help thinking that yes, Lissa had a key. But so did Philpott Peabody. He was, after all, still a member of the department. He must have had an office in the building, and, surely he had a key.

"Now the ball is in your court," she said. "I told you all of these things. Now you know. The rest is up to you. You've got to get her arrested! She's a murderess."

Wearily, I repeated that I had no role in the affair whatsoever. That unleashed another torrent of words, and then she stormed out with Philpott trailing behind her. I breathed a sigh of relief and went back to work.

But, to my surprise, about half an hour later Peabody returned. I was sitting in my office, peacefully working, when I heard a knock on the door. I opened it and there he was. "Mr. May?" he asked, in his timid voice.

"Yes?"

"I want to talk to you. Explain some things. Do you have a moment?"

"I'm kind of busy ..."

"It won't take long," he said. "Mrs. Hardcastle has an appointment with her doctor. She has high blood pressure. It's a worry. She's not in great health, and the strain of these events ... I try to take care of her. Mr. May, people don't understand her. She's a diamond in the rough. They only see the rough."

It was, indeed, all I could see. "Call me Frank," I said.

He nodded his head, and told me to call him Phil. He went on, "Anyway, I've learned to appreciate her. Many people don't. You know the saying, 'beauty is only skin deep.' It's not even that. It's a social construct, like gender. I believe that. The eye sees what it wants to see, what society tells it to see. I try to get past that. That's why I went in for psychology; so I could get past surfaces, you know, get to the essence of things. And things do have essences. In the past, I worked closely with Ramsey and I was his assistant on his projects.

"One night, he had me over to the house for dinner, and that's where I met Mildred. She's a striking woman, you have to admit. I found her ... fascinating. She's amazingly intelligent, and she seemed to take an interest in me. Ramsey became quite jealous. They were not getting along, it was a marriage made in hell, so why did he care? Mildred confided in me," he said, lowering his voice to a whisper, "about the professor's sexual habits. They were pretty bizarre. I knew this marriage wasn't going to last and, in fact, I told her, 'You shouldn't stay another minute with that man, he's poison. He doesn't deserve you.'"

Where was this going?

"I was in a terrible position," he said. "Ramsey is a power-house. In the field, in the profession, and most certainly in the department. The chair of the department, Dr. Edelweiss, is a weakling, an absolute weakling, and he wraps her around his fingers. I was up for tenure, you see, and Ramsey made it very clear that I wasn't going to get it. He used every dirty trick in the book and, in addition, he let it be known that any vote to give me tenure would be over his dead body. Oh dear, I didn't mean that the way it sounds! That phrase about the dead body."

"It's okay," I said, but I had to wonder. Ramsey Hardcastle was a dead body now, after all.

"I don't know how much you know about the tenure process," he continued. "They review your work and they also get letters from experts, for example, professors at other schools. Ramsey made sure they got bad letters, letters criticizing my work. Prejudiced, narrow-minded people, or people under his thumb. I'm very proud of my work. But you can't fight a man like Ramsey Hardcastle. He held all the cards. I lost that fight. I'm going to have to look for another job and it is all Ramsey's fault."

"I'm sorry to hear that," I said.

"I'm looking," he said, "but so far, no luck. Any place that was interested, of course they'd consult the great man, and he would tell them not to hire me. Maybe things will be easier now."

Easier, right—because he's dead, I thought, and dead men can't do slander.

"Anybody with an open mind," he said, "would see that my work is interesting, innovative, solid. I study the connection between anger and lust. Ramsey thought he was the world's greatest expert on anger; thought he owned it, if you know what I mean. And some of his recent work was about lust. That's why I came here, to work with him.

"That was before I knew what a bastard he was. I had grants. I had a great project and recruited students as subjects. The male students would look at pictures of naked women, beautiful women, and the women would look at pictures of naked men, handsome, athletic men. Then they were supposed to fill out a questionnaire—that's what we would tell them, along with some phony story about what we were testing, and why. Meanwhile, they begin looking at these pictures, and suddenly, the screen gets blurred, or the video goes blank, and they get all frustrated and angry, that's the whole point. They think it's mechanical failure, but it isn't. It's part of the experiment. Oh yes, and with some of the groups, the naked woman morphs into an ugly, aged one, with skinny breasts that sort of hang down, and the men morph into old geezers, with big fat stomachs and tiny shriveled-up penises, and we measure the subjects' reactions and how they respond to questions. It's all about lust, anger, and the connection between these two things.

"Oh yes, and I had a plan that after this phase we would try the same experiment with gay people, and then transgender people—you know, men who think they're really women, and women who think they're really men. I would have to tweak the experiment. But Ramsey told me this whole plan was no good, it couldn't be done, and that the Institutional Review Board would never agree. Of course, though he didn't say it, I knew he would make darn sure that the Board turned me down.

"You know what? I think he was going to do the study himself. Change it a little, to fool NSF, or maybe not even fool them—he has buddies there, he's a famous guy—and he could trample all over me. He'd use his influence on the Board too. That man had no sense of ethics. None at all. He didn't care that he ruined my life; that meant nothing to him. He's ruined many lives, I'm sure."

I couldn't help thinking: In front of me is a young man, Philpott Peabody, who has a genuine, strong motive for killing Ramsey Hardcastle. Maybe he thought he could get tenure if Hardcastle was out of the way. Or maybe he knew it would smooth the way for a new position at some other university. Or maybe he acted out of pure hatred and revenge. If so, was

Mildred in on it? She hated Ramsey. And they were together that night. Now, of course, they're trying to put all the blame on Lissa. Did Philpott not realize how much he was damning *himself*?

"Why am I telling you all this?" he said. "I want you to know what kind of a man he was. The world is better off without him. Not that I approve of killing people. I'm a pacifist. I'm vegan, too. I never touch meat, or dairy products, because I respect the lives of all animals. But you should know, Frank, that the woods are full of people who are glad he's dead— people who might have accelerated the process, if you know what I mean."

"Who, for instance?"

"I'm not going to give you names," he said. "I've talked to the police. They can follow up. There are people he cheated all over the world. Scholars. Members of the department." He lowered his voice to a whisper, "A musician, even. A violinist. He hated Ramsey Hardcastle."

"A musician? For God's sake, why?"

"I can't tell you," he said, in his low, conspiratorial voice.

Soon after that, he left. I wasn't sure what to make of all this. I guess he was trying to make a point. But why me? It must have been because of this ridiculous notion that I was somehow involved as a detective, or an investigator, or whatever—or maybe simply an officious meddler. And the point of the visit? To shift suspicion away from his beloved Mildred.

Or himself. He had to be a suspect. Philpott, more than anyone else, had a real motive, a real reason to kill Ramsey Hardcastle, nothing bizarre and far-fetched, but a reason that was concrete, immediate, and strong.

Still, I had trouble thinking of Philpott Peabody as a cold-blooded killer. He had a Ph.D. in psychology and was a skinny man, with bony fingers and an Adam's apple that bobbed up and down when he talked. It just didn't figure. But of course I could be wrong. I often am.

And what was this talk about a musician? Philpott refused to say. Could this be a reference to a Hungarian musician? And would I ever find out what this was all about?

15

The day after this meeting with Mildred and Philpott, I got a call from Sylvan. He said, "I really enjoyed our lunch. We should get together more often. Most people I know just grab a sandwich, or fast food; it's a pity. I know they're busy, but, hey, what's life for anyway? I get the impression you love to eat, like me. I mean, not just fuel, not just something to keep the furnace going, but one of the joys of life. That's what it is, Frank."

"You bet," I said.

"I know a place that features molecular food, would you give it a try?"

"'Molecular food,' Sylvan? What on earth is that? I mean, isn't everything made up of molecules—food, too, no? French fries, asparagus, everything."

"No, no, of course that's true, but molecular cooking is a style. There's this restaurant in Palo Alto, downtown Palo Alto. It's gotten rave reviews and I'm dying to go. It's a scientific way of cooking. Real science, you know, physics, chemistry. They have these wonderful dishes. I read about it. The paper had one of their recipes. They boil mustard and dandelion leaves and make a kind of froth out of it, foamy, so that it's, well, like cotton candy—I don't mean the taste, I mean the texture—and then they mix it with caviar and foie gras and the whole thing is steamed in a special machine and served on a special plate, and all that, and pressed into the shape of a butterfly, with little tiny colored things put in like the butterfly's eyes and so on. So realistic, you can even tell what species it is, if you're a butterfly expert. Supposed to be totally delicious. But I have to tell you, it's ferociously expensive. Hundreds of dollars. But we're making money, aren't we, Frank?"

"Maybe you are, Sylvan. I'm not. I mean, I'm making a living, but I have to be careful; I have two teenaged daughters. They'll go to college, I hope, and do you know what that costs these days? An arm and a leg."

"Tell me about it," he said. "I've been down that road."

"Sylvan, frankly, lunch for hundreds of dollars? Unless I had a client paying for it ... no thanks."

"Okay, we'll do something else. Anyway, lunch isn't why I called, Frank. I mean it is, but it's not the only reason. I wanted to tell you something new about Ramsey Hardcastle."

"Oh? Something new? What is it, Sylvan?"

"I can't talk now. I'll tell you at lunch. Are you available?"

I was definitely available. We agreed to meet in Redwood City, at a nice restaurant I recommended, which was not at all molecular, and therefore priced more reasonably. It was upscale Italian. None of the dishes looked like identifiable butterflies, but they were nonetheless delicious. Sylvan ate with his usual gusto.

"You know, I made out his will," he said, "Ramsey's will. Or, to be more precise, he had a living trust, and the will is a pour-over. You know what I'm talking about; you've done it dozens of times. Of course, he was married, and that's a complication, but he assured me the divorce was coming very soon. Anyway, when he signed the documents, I told him he could change his arrangements anytime he wanted to. You know the drill, Frank. So he said, 'How do I do that?' And I said, 'Easy as pie, you just let me know, and I'll draw up the papers.' But, maybe he was stingy and didn't want to pay. Anyway, he said, 'Well what if I'm in a huge hurry? Can't wait?' I said, 'Why Ramsey, what's the rush? You planning on dying?' He didn't even smile—the man had no sense of humor, I should have known better—I slapped him on the back and said, 'You're going to live forever, Ramsey.' All he did was grunt. But I said, 'Okay, you can change the trust, but you have to do it a certain way, look at paragraph so-and-so on page whatever.' And he said, 'I don't like that.' So we changed the clause, letting him do it in the same way you'd do a holographic will. I explained what that was. 'Just take out a piece of paper, and write what you want. But write it, don't type it. And for God's sake, put on a date, so we know when you did it. But please, Ramsey, it's not a good idea. Just let me know if you want to make a change; it's not a do-it-yourself project.' And he nodded his head, and I forgot all about it. And guess what?"

"He actually did it."

"Damn right. After he died, this daughter of his flew in from wherever she was living. Jennifer Hardcastle. She couldn't stand him, by the way, but now that he was dead, she smelled money. Funny the way the smell of money affects people. She was going through his papers, and she found an envelope, a sealed envelope, with the word 'amendment to living trust' on the outside. And she opened it. You know, I happened to be there at the time, otherwise she would have just torn the darn thing up. But I said, 'What've you got there?' And here was this handwritten note inside: 'I hereby amend my trust as follows, on my death, one-third of my estate goes to Lissa King.' That was all. Oh yes, and his signature. And the date, shortly before he was killed, a day or two before.

"The daughter, she's really bitchy, she said, 'What is this?' And I said, 'We have something called a holographic will in California and that's what this is—it's an amendment to his trust—and it's basically the same as a will.' And she was scowling, and she said, 'Well, it isn't legal, is it? It's got no witnesses.' And I said, 'I'm afraid it is legal.' And she looked as if she was going to have a cow. But that's interesting, isn't it? How about that? You know what people said about this Lissa. Mind you, I don't know her. But you have to wonder what their relationship was. You don't leave all that money to a secretary. Unless she's more than a secretary. I don't have to draw you a picture. This is definitely a complication."

That was certainly true. I had to wonder, why this sudden generosity toward Lissa King? *Were* they having an affair? And did she know about Ramsey's plan to leave her money? It would give her a motive for killing the guy. If she knew about it.

Of course, if she did kill him, she couldn't inherit; that's in the Probate Code. But people don't think of those things.

I remembered my distinct feeling about Lissa; that she was lying to me about something. Lying to me, and probably to the police. But exactly what she was lying about—that was the question. About her relationship with Ramsey Hardcastle? About the money? Or about something else.

"This estate," Sylvan said, "is a colossal pain in the butt. If I get through this alive, so to speak, and get a big fee, I'll treat you to a molecular lunch. But don't hold your breath."

16

Of course, I wasn't investigating these two murders, but I *was* intrigued by them. It seemed to me there were at least three hot suspects. One was Lissa King. But you couldn't leave out Mildred and Philpott. Then, to my surprise, I found another suspect. Who, you ask? Ah, there's the rub. He didn't even have a name. At least not then.

The source of this new suspect was Teddy. He came to my office, on his bike, as usual, and waited patiently in the hallway while I discussed a living trust with one of my clients, a middle-aged woman who had inherited two small car wash companies from her late husband. I had to listen to her endless complaints about her son-in-law, soon to be her ex-son-in-law. "The way he treats my daughter!" she said, "He's filthy rich, but he doesn't want to part with a penny." I explained to her—as patiently as I could—a number of plans we could draw up to take care of her daughter, financially speaking. She seemed to listen—they always seem to listen—and then went right back to her screed about the young man in question. She was full of hatred. Then she mentioned, in passing, that her daughter, Felicity, had been sleeping with a deliveryman she met when he brought in a new living room sofa. This was before the breakup. Did she really think Felicity's behavior had nothing to do with her son-in-law's attitude, that he was simply a cad?

When we were finally done, and the client left, Teddy came in pushing his bike.

"You cutting class again?" I said.

"Whatever. There are more important things. Anyway, I

told the teacher I had a toothache, I said it was killing me and I had to go to the dentist."

"Teddy, you shouldn't lie."

"Hey, Mr. May, everybody lies. Show me somebody who doesn't lie. This was English lit. I like the course, most of the time. We did *Julius Caesar* and acted it out. The teacher's great. She's really fun, sometimes. But then we started reading this book, *The Mill on the Floss*. Booooring. I mean, I think Shakespeare's terrific, you have to work at it—read the footnotes—but when you act it out, it's okay, really. We all had to read parts, you know. Omar was Brutus. I said, 'Omar, you couldn't act your way out of a paper bag.' I mean, he read the lines with no expression whatsoever. I said, 'You got to put some *emotion* into it, it's not a grocery list, know what I mean?' Anyway, this *Mill on the Floss* thing, who cares? It's the worst thing I ever read. Or started to read. I gave up around page 10. I'll look it up on Google and find out the plot, and then I don't have to read it. I'm getting an A in this class anyway. Teacher loves me. So I'm not worried."

"Teddy," I said, "I'm not interested in your English teacher. What on earth are you doing here?"

"I think I got a lead. I'm talking about the murder case. The one in the Williams house."

"A lead? What kind of a lead?"

"I've been doing some research, you know? Trying to find out stuff. Do you need somebody to help you? I mean, I'd love to do it. For money. I like money, I want to get things, I want to buy a new bike, a guitar, stuff like that; Mom doesn't have a lot of money, that's for sure. It's okay, my mom's awesome, I'm not complaining. But I know she worries about money. My friend Buzz, like, his dad is in some kind of computer apps business and they have this big house and lots of money. He's got his own car, even. Wish I had a car. Even an old beat-up car. I said to Mom once, 'Hey, I looked up our house on the web, you can find out what things are worth—and this house, you could sell it for a zillion dollars.' She said, 'But where would we live?' And she loves the house, she really does. And we'd have to move someplace else, like the East Bay, or the Central Valley, where it's a thousand degrees in the summer—you could die there—and the kids are all dorks. Anyway, okay, I'm talking too much. But do you need an assistant?"

"No Teddy, I don't," I said. "And, Teddy, even if I did, it's not a job for you. You have to go to school, get the grades, get into college. The police, they're the ones who are working on this case. It's their job. Besides, do you ever stop to think that it might be dangerous? After all, there's a killer out there, right? Maybe he doesn't want to be investigated. I haven't noticed anybody confessing. Do you get my point, Teddy?"

"You trying to scare me, Mr. May? Okay, you did scare me. But it's not like I could just say 'Oh, forget it.' I can't. Because of that key. I had the key to the house. Had it on me. Nobody else had it. So, this is about me, right? I mean, I'm a suspect, no?"

"Teddy, be serious. Nobody thinks you killed that woman."

"Not me—but, here's the question, who did? My mom? Yeah, she could kill somebody; I really think so, like if somebody was messing with me, you know, kidnapping me or whatever. But, I don't think it's my mom. I think it's a guy she had a date with. Somebody she found on some website. You know, that's what people do, they look for people on these websites. You have to pay something, I think. Anyway, after you pay, I guess you send a picture or something. Half the time it's a fake. Then you talk about who you are. Mom does that. She's embarrassed and she doesn't like me to know about it. But she wants to meet guys. I mean, she's lonely, you can't blame her. And so she got together with this guy. He comes to the house, and stuff. So here's what I'm thinking, *he* got the key."

"He got the key? How? And who is this guy?"

"I don't know his name, but I know what he looks like. I'm going to try to find out, like, who he is. Younger guy. Mom, like I said, it's something she's sort of ashamed of—I mean, she shouldn't be, she's got to have a life, too—anyway, I was home, and he came to pick her up, to take her to a movie or something. When she came home, I said, 'Mom, what're you doing? This guy is young enough to be your kid.' She started crying, saying stuff about how there was nothing to it, just company. I said, 'Hold on, Mom, don't get upset. I was just talking. It's not like you're gonna marry this guy.' She said, 'Oh, no Teddy, I would never do that. But he's nice, he's nice to be with.' So she saw him again. And I think he spent the night. I was asleep when they came in, they were out really late. That's when he must have got the key."

"Teddy, you told me that couldn't really happen."

"Yeah, I did. Look, I told you, I sleep with the key on. Now here's a fact, I sleep real sound when I'm asleep, and nobody and nothing can wake me—an earthquake, nothing, I mean, the house could burn down—that's the truth. The guys make fun of me because when I spent the night at Omar's, and I had been bragging about how I sleep, and I went to sleep first—I was real tired for some reason—and I was in a sleeping bag in Omar's room, and Omar and Buzz came in, and they were tickling me and doing all sorts of stuff—punching me, making loud noises, and they couldn't wake me—and finally, they poured a glass of water on me, and boy, did that wake me up, I said, 'What the fuck is going on here?' pardon my language ..."

"Teddy, what are you saying? This guy came in, took the key, and then what?"

"Made a copy, I suppose. Put the key back. Maybe my mom was asleep, who knows? He must have known this was the key to that house, maybe my mom told him, 'Teddy is looking after this house,' whatever. Here's what I figure: This guy, he had a plan, he was gonna kill this woman. Maybe she was somebody who had some dirt on him, blackmail, you know ..."

"Blackmail? Why blackmail?"

"Hey, suppose, just suppose, he meets women—older women, see? They're lonely and he finds out stuff, and who knows? They tell him secrets, or they give him money. But there's this one woman, she's got the goods on him, they're lovers, say, but he doesn't trust her, and he decides she's got to go. Anyway, this guy, he goes out with my mom and he finds out I've got this key, and he thinks, 'Aha! Someplace to stash the body when I do this thing.' So he's got this copy of the key, and the next day, say he goes ahead and does it—kills this woman—then it gets dark and nobody can see what's going on, so he comes with the key, opens the door, and puts the body in that chest or trunk or whatever you want to call it."

Well, it was possible, I suppose. It was a possible scenario. But extremely unlikely. I just couldn't picture it—it seemed so clumsy. So improbable. I told Teddy it was just too farfetched. But Teddy was totally excited about the prospect.

"My mom, she refused to tell me who he was. She said, 'Forget about him,' she says, 'You're the biggest thing in my life, Teddy, and I love you,' blah blah ... I mean, I don't want to make fun, she does love me—maybe too much, sometimes I have to say, 'Cut it out, Mom, stop kissing me and spoiling me, I'm not a baby'—anyway, she says, 'If you don't want me to, I won't ever see that guy again.' I said, 'Why—you mad at him Mom?' And she said, 'No, no, he was awfully nice.' 'Well, then,' I said, 'did he do something bad?' And she said, 'Oh, Teddy, really, please, you're embarrassing me. I told you; he was really nice, a nice guy, sweet, don't get the wrong idea. It's just that ... he's so young ...' And then I had to say, 'Aw, Ma, stop it,' because she was crying and crying. I felt like a rat. I said, 'Okay, Mom, it's okay, whatever you want.'

"But then I thought: She thinks he's so nice, but maybe he's a killer, I don't want her mixed up with a killer, it's like she's in danger. I mean, he could be all sweet and lovey-dovey, but he's got something to hide. What do you think?"

"Teddy, I have no idea. Do you think she still sees him?"

"I know she does. In a sneaky way, mostly. Because of me. And it's got to be him. It's just got to."

"Why Teddy?"

"Hey, who else? I mean, if somebody used the key. My mom—like I told you—it couldn't be her. And it's not me, that's for sure. So it's him. I mean, it could be, right? Don't you think it *could* be him?"

Naturally, I refused to commit myself. I told Teddy I had no idea, since I didn't know the man or anything about him, and I had some advice for Teddy: stick to the schoolbooks and "try to control your vivid imagination."

"Sure thing, Mr. May." He nodded, and sailed off with his bike. But the way he nodded, and the look on his face gave me an unmistakable message. He was definitely not about to control that vivid imagination. No, he was going to "look into things," as he said once. He would keep chasing his theory.

* * *

I told the whole story to Celia. She seemed unusually interested. Of course, I stressed how good I had been, how distant I kept myself from the whole sordid affair; and the excellent advice I gave Teddy. She seemed satisfied.

But, to my great surprise, Celia brought the subject up herself two days later. We were sitting in the living room, after dinner. I was reading a book; Celia was knitting. The girls were in their rooms.

Celia reminded me that she was good friends with a woman who lived down the block, Clarissa Bankman. Clarissa taught social studies at one of the local high schools—she and Celia loved to share tales of woe about students, administrators, and the general low state of public education. "You know, Frank," she said, "you're not the only one around here who can play great detective."

"Oh, come on, honey, you're teasing me. I'm behaving myself, and you know it."

"You are and you aren't. You don't fool me for a minute, Frank. Anyway, Clarissa Bankman—you know her, the one with the mole on her chin—she's in the same book group with Tina Gilchrist. Everybody remembered the day after they found the body. It was a Sunday night and by Monday everybody knew the story and, as you can imagine, the whole neighborhood was buzzing. At the book group, they were all saying, 'Where were you that day?' and so on, and 'When did you hear about it?' and they were specifically interested, of course, in Tina—especially when she told them she knew something about this business— and they kept quizzing her, until they got her to tell them about Teddy and the key, and then they said, 'Oh, Tina, of course you and your boy had nothing to do with it. Just out of curiosity, where were you and where was Teddy on that Sunday?' and she said, 'Well Teddy was at a friend's house, and I was home, all by myself. I had things to do, bills to pay, and so on.' But Clarissa says she was lying."

"Lying? How would she know?"

"Oh, Clarissa said, yes, Tina was home alright; but not by herself. Because she, Clarissa, walked by at, oh, maybe two o'clock in the afternoon, and she saw a man come out of the house, a young man, and kind of good-looking. He got into a car and drove off. Clarissa didn't say anything about it. She said, 'Tina's a nice woman, and she's divorced, raising a boy all by herself, she's entitled to have men come over, and maybe he was a salesman or something, who knows?'"

"Doesn't mean a thing," I said. "Don't you agree?"

"Well, why did she lie?"

"She was embarrassed. Didn't want to admit she had a gentleman caller."

"Maybe. I don't think she had anything to do with this murder, although how would I know? People do strange things. I do think she knows more than she's letting on. Teddy's theory isn't quite so crazy as it sounds. Maybe his mother is an accomplice. She got the key, and she made a copy. And then she gave the key to this guy. He killed the woman, and dumped her in the house—maybe when it got dark, but before the Williams' arrived."

I was amazed. This was a new side of Celia. Did she really believe what she was saying? I think she was just having fun with me. "But this seems so complicated," I said. "Why would this guy do all this, in this crazy way? Anyway, we don't even know who he is."

Celia was quiet for a minute. I heard the knitting needles clicking. Then she said, "Frank, I have no idea. None whatsoever. But maybe there was something funny going on, something we just don't know about. And this man, or somebody else, could have gotten the key when Teddy was asleep, or in the shower."

"But there's no motive," I said. "There's got to be a motive. People don't just kill. In Agatha Christie and other stories like hers, you need to find a motive. Then you can solve the case. That's what they do in those books."

"This is life, Frank, not books. Now I've got to concentrate on my knitting. I'm making a sweater for Adam Finkel; the poor man has nothing decent to wear. And he seems so depressed."

I doubted whether a sweater would cure the depression of this lonely math teacher, but you couldn't blame Celia for trying.

17

I didn't know Tina Gilchrist, but somehow I couldn't imagine her as a killer. Or a killer's accomplice. Teddy Gilchrist's mother? It seemed impossible.

Despite my great advice to Teddy, the day after my conversation with Celia, as I was working in my office in the late afternoon, there he was again in my hallway, pushing his bicycle. I said, "Teddy, you're cutting class again? Another toothache?"

"I'm legit today. No class. Something to do with teachers, teacher improvement, I don't know. We got the day off. Hey, listen, I found out more about the guy."

"What guy?"

"The guy my mom was seeing. I know she's still seeing him. And I said, 'Mom, look, it's okay, this guy's a friend, you don't have to hide him from me. But I got to ask you, Mom, who is he, what does he do?' So she said, 'Teddy, really, why do you need to know?' I said, 'Well, if he's going to be my stepdad ...' and she said, 'Get out of here! What's gotten into you, young man? Nobody's going to be your stepdad.' 'Well,' I said, 'then tell me his name.' She went, 'Teddy, really, you're embarrassing me, he's just a friend.' I went, 'Sure, but why can't you tell me? Who is this friend?' She said, 'Well, his name is Griffin.' I said, 'Okay, that's a name, but what else? I mean, Mom, you don't want to keep secrets from me, do you?' So she said, 'Oh Teddy ...' and she got all flustered and I said, 'Come on, Mom, what's the big deal?' And she said, 'You're right, okay, it's no secret ... he's some kind of graduate student or he's on a fellowship or something like that,' and I said, 'What kind, what department, you know, is it law or medicine or some kind of engineering?' And she says, 'No, no, psychology.' 'Yeah, what kind of psychology?' She says, 'I don't know, really,' but here's the funny part—he was actually working for this big-shot professor—the one who was murdered—and Griffin, he was very upset as you can imagine."

I had to admit: this was a stunning coincidence. If it was a coincidence at all. I don't really believe in coincidences.

"So you see, Mr. May, I just gotta be right. She says he's nice, and he's just a friend, but why is he hanging around my mom? To get the key from me. And look, he had a connection with this psych prof too; maybe he's the one that killed that guy. Maybe my mom doesn't realize who this guy is. I mean, he's sweet and friendly—but it's all an act. Like I said, maybe he's a young guy who looks for older women and he takes advantage of them. Tell you the truth, I'm a little scared for my mom. Maybe she's dating some kind of nut."

"Teddy," I said, "I don't think your mom is in any kind of danger. You're letting your imagination run away with you."

"Hey, Mr. May, really," he said. "You have to admit, it's peculiar, I mean, this psychology department business. And I have this feeling—somebody's been watching me. It's kind of exciting, in a way, I mean, I'm not really scared, but it's creepy. I told the guys about it—Buzz and Omar—and they said I was crazy in the head. But maybe someone *is* following me. Or, could be that somebody's listening in, wiretap or whatever, or maybe the CIA is getting my texts, I mean, we text all day long, you know, me and the guys. We went to Buzz's aunt's house, real nice lady, and she gave us pasta for dinner and then I went for a walk—the other guys were watching some stuff on TV, but I didn't want to, you know, I ate too much—I said, hey, I need some fresh air, and I swear, somebody was following me."

"Oh, come on Teddy, really. Why would anybody follow you around?"

"It's because of this case, you know, the dead woman and now the professor. I had the key to the house, it all fits in, you know? They think I know something. And maybe I do. Only I don't know what it is that I know. So anyway, they're following me around."

"Teddy, I don't believe it."

He shrugged his shoulders. "Man, as I said, I'm not scared, but it's getting to me. I keep thinking, who's out there, and what's their angle? I started doing some research, you know? On the web, about this professor—the one who got killed. He's been married four times, did you know that? He's on his fourth wife. Lissa told me about her. Lissa likes to talk to me, to tell me her troubles and she's real upset, as you can imagine. So we were talking about things. She says this woman, the professor's wife; she's a crazy person. They were separated. Okay, so maybe she was crazy jealous. Maybe she knew the professor was doing stuff with somebody else, sex stuff, and then she got really jealous and angry, and she goes, well, 'If I can't have him, nobody will,' and she kills him—that's what I think."

"Well, Teddy, that's a new theory. What happened to the old theory, about your mom's friend? Did you give up on that?"

"Naw, no way. I'm just thinking about different possibilities, you know? I like this one, this idea, anyway—it lets my mom off the hook. This crazy woman killed the professor. It makes sense, don't you think?"

"But, Teddy, what about Lissa's sister? And the body in Margot Williams' house?"

"Well, I don't know where that fits in. But there's got to be a connection, I mean, there has to be."

"I think so too, but still: look, I talked to the professor—he came to see me—and he said he didn't even know this woman, his secretary's sister ... never met her. That's what he said."

"Yeah, but he could be lying, Mr. May. I mean, maybe they were having sex, you know, on the side, and he likes it rough, let's say, and he got a little too enthusiastic—if you know what I mean—maybe he's one of those people who do kooky things, and they're trying out something new, and, first thing you know, she's dead and he has to get rid of the body ..."

"Kooky things?"

"I mean, she was strangled, didn't they say that? Maybe that's part of the deal—there's this guy in high school, and there are rumors, the girls talk about him, he's a little bit off, you know, in the sex department, and the rumors are about this one girl, she's basically a slut, and she went out with this guy, and things happened—you know what I mean."

"I know what you mean, Teddy. Or I think I do. But you're just making stuff up. Without a shred of evidence. You know, we lawyers, we like evidence. Real evidence. You're saying the professor killed the girl, and then his wife killed him—but where's the evidence?"

"It could be, couldn't it? This woman, this kook, she could have done it, no? I mean, she's a total nut case, that's what Lissa said. And maybe she's the one who's following me around."

I knew it was pointless to talk him out of this particular fear. I said, "Teddy, nobody's following you. And anyway, most of the time you're riding a bike, aren't you? How could somebody follow you, least of all, this lady? She's old, Teddy, she's fat, and I can't imagine her on a bicycle."

"Hey, that's a good point!" he said on his way out.

* * *

I often go into the office on a Saturday to catch up on paperwork. But that weekend I stayed at home, just relaxing. I went for a long walk in the morning, and then tried to catch up on my magazine reading, especially the *National Geographics*, piling up on our coffee table. When I'm tired, every once in a while, I browse through them looking at photographs of walruses or cheetahs, or an account of the life of some obscure group of people in Siberia, who live on whale blubber or whatever and, despite the text, which is often rather sympathetic to their way of life, I have to wonder how any human being could live in such places. This time, I was deep into a story about piranhas—those terrible little fish with sharp teeth—that eat anything that foolishly invades their stretch of the Amazon, including people I suppose. I was half finished when the doorbell range. Celia said, "Frank, would you see who that is?"

In suburbia, absolutely nobody rings your doorbell unless you invited them to come over and were expecting them. There are almost never any surprises, unless it's Jehovah's Witnesses with their magazine, or a college student with a petition about the plight of the sperm whale. I opened the door, and said, "Yes?" to a middle-aged woman. She said, "I'm Tina Gilchrist. I hate to disturb you at home, but I wondered if I could come in and talk to you for a few minutes."

There was nothing I wanted less to do, but I put down the magazine I was reading and I said, "Sure," and invited her in. Celia emerged from the kitchen and I introduced her to Tina. I had talked enough about the case so that Celia knew who she was. "Can I offer you some coffee, or tea?" Celia asked.

"Oh, that would be nice. Tea, please. But herbal tea, if you have it."

The tea idea suggested that Tina would be longer than a "few minutes," but there are rules about hospitality.

She was a woman of 50 or so, of average height and weight, with grey hair and a round, rather friendly face. She was neatly dressed. I noticed she had no rings on any of her fingers. "I want to talk to you about my Teddy," she said. "I know he comes to see you—he cuts classes—I found out about it. I wish he wouldn't do that."

"I don't encourage it," I said. "I absolutely don't. I tell him, 'Teddy, you should be in school.'"

She had a serious look on her face, and suddenly, she was crying. Softly. A few big tears, rolling down her cheek. Celia brought in the tea, and stared at Tina, asking, "Is something wrong?"

"My boy," she said. "He's all I've got. There's just the two of us. He's a good boy, Teddy. He gets good grades in school, he has good friends, I can't complain. And he works hard, he's ambitious. He tries to make a little extra money, and I tell him, 'You don't have to do that, Teddy,' but he wants to. Now though, this awful business ... the dead body ... He came and talked to me, and I could see he was upset—I can read my boy like a book. So I said, 'Teddy, what's on your mind?' He said, 'Mother, this guy who comes here, who is he? And do you trust him?' He was referring to a friend of mine, a young man—we go to the movies sometimes, and have coffee—that's all. And then he told me this fantastic story about the key and how he was sure the man had gotten hold of the key, and he said, 'Maybe he's dangerous, you know, I'm worried about you.' And he told me all about his conversations with you, so I thought, I really have to talk to the lawyer, Frank May, and that's why I'm here. I hope I'm not intruding. I just want to explain things."

Celia was listening to every word. And I could tell, from the look on her face, that Tina Gilchrist had won her total sympathy.

"I'm a single mom," Tina said. "And it's a lonely life. This man, the one Teddy was talking to you about, he's just a friend, really—maybe it could be more than that, but I don't think so. And, anyway, it isn't going to continue. He's a kind, sweet young man, and ... I enjoy his company. I mean, I did. I won't see him any more if it troubles Teddy. This story about the key, I just don't believe it. Really, there's no way my friend could have taken it. No, only Teddy had the key, and he's super conscientious; it was never out of his sight. I just wanted to come and explain all this to you."

She dabbed at her eyes again. I said, "Don't be upset. I'm sure you're right. But did Teddy tell you in particular *why* he was suspicious of your friend? It was because of his connection with Stanford, with the psychology department."

"Oh," she said, "that's just a coincidence. Or maybe not really ... Teddy thinks I met him because of some website—and I have done that sort of thing—but I met Griffin, that's his name, Griffin Peabody, I met him on the street. It was actually rather sweet, something out of a Hollywood movie. I had been in the supermarket and I was going home. It was raining, I didn't have an umbrella, and I slipped, and the bags fell on the street, you know—apples were rolling around on the street—and he came by and helped me. He picked me up, picked up the groceries, and we started talking. He knew Lissa, he said, I think maybe he tried to date her (he's in the psychology department some sort of post-graduate student, or an assistant), and he's a cousin of somebody who worked for the professor who was murdered.

"Anyway, I couldn't thank him enough, and he was soaking wet, and so was I, so I invited him to the house. It was close by, and I offered to give him something hot to drink, and he said, 'Sure,' and we started talking. He told me all about his life, and his troubles, and, well, we became friends."

Celia was nodding her head; she seemed quite taken with this woman. Tina seemed like a decent person, but I had trouble concentrating on what she was saying. My foot had fallen asleep, and I had a headache. I desperately wanted to escape and this seemed impossible. Celia went into the kitchen and came back with a blue and white teapot—our most elegant teapot, and one she rarely took from the cupboard. She also brought a tray of pastries. Tina had clearly made a hit with her.

Celia's attitude puzzled me a little. I found out why, but only after Tina had gone.

"Isn't she nice?" Celia said. "I really liked her."

"Seems nice enough, yes."

"Frank, dear, I was thinking, what about Adam? Adam Finkel?"

"What about him?"

"I know she's a bit older than he is ..."

"A bit?" I said. "Could be a good 10 years."

"Oh, I don't think so. I think she's in her 40's, don't you? Well, maybe a bit older. Poor Adam is so shy; I think the young women scare him. I mentioned the woman in P.E., the one we just hired—but that's not going to work. Turns out she has a live-in boyfriend. Anyway, Tina is lonely, and nice, and he's lonely and nice. I'd like to invite her for dinner, and have Adam over too, just to see what happens. What do you think?"

Of course, I thought it was a terrible idea. This wouldn't be the first of these dinners, and they had all been disasters. But I knew better than to say so. Celia was off and running: "I'll invite her boy too. He's just the right age for our girls, isn't he? They might like meeting him."

Teddy did seem much nicer than the boys my daughters occasionally dragged home. They were uniformly sullen and scruffy, had ridiculous hair, and obviously considered parents subhuman, or members of a different, alien species. But I knew this part of the plan was doomed from the start. The mere fact that we, the parents, had invited this boy over would be enough to sink his ship as far as my daughters were concerned.

Celia, however, was bound and determined, and she didn't waste time. She called Tina the next day, told her what a nice chat they had had, and wouldn't she and her son like to come for dinner? She named a day, and Tina accepted. She then called Adam, and he, too, was willing to come.

The first sign of trouble was on the home front. My daughters, as predicted, flatly refused to have anything to do with this dinner party. They normally stay away from such things and when their mother told them she'd really like them to be home for this one—a Mrs. Gilchrist is coming with her son, he's 17, and he's an awfully nice young man—that, as I feared, was the kiss of death. They said, "No, no, no. You people are from the dark ages."

I tried to help out. "Well, of course, it's your choice, but your mother and I would like you to be there." They flatly refused. I could see there was no chance of persuading them or making them come, short of a flat-out parental order, backed by possible sanctions. But taking this step was like exploding a nuclear weapon; it could only be used in the direst of circumstances, and this dinner hardly seemed to justify this move.

That was the first intimation of disaster. Poor Celia. Getting a woman for Adam Finkel was her way of tilting at windmills. I knew in my heart that this was never going to work.

The date was fixed for Sunday night. Teddy and his mother came promptly at seven. She brought a bottle of red wine and a bunch of tulips. Teddy looked ill at ease. He was wearing chino pants, and running shoes instead of flip-flops. They sat down in the living room; Celia brought out a dish of cheese and crackers, and a small bowl of nuts.

The doorbell rang, and Adam came in. Teddy stared at him. Tina took a look, and then glanced away. Celia introduced them: "Adam, this is a friend of ours, Tina Gilchrist, and her son, Teddy." Tina couldn't help looking at his face—poor man, at his awful skin, all lumps and bumps, finished off with an angry red blotch—and he blushed. Then she looked away, and tried to pretend she hadn't seen anything. They sat in the living room and nibbled at cheese. Adam said very little. Tina, like her son, was a talker. She said, "You teach math, don't you? Celia mentioned that. I always liked math in school. My boy Teddy, he doesn't like math; he's a good student, but he says, math gives him a rash." Adam blushed even worse, and looked distinctly unhappy. "Oh dear," she said, "did I say something wrong ... I didn't mean ... about the rash ..."

"It's okay," Adam said.

Tina proceeded, poor woman, to dig herself in deeper. "I have a brother, Jesse," she said, "he's a dermatologist, one of the best. He's at the Palo Alto clinic, and he's also something or other at Stanford Hospital. He does research, maybe he could help, I don't mean to pry, but ... I could give you his name ..."

"Tina, could you come in the kitchen for a minute and help me with something," Celia said. Tina said, "Excuse me," and went into the kitchen. In fact, Celia never wants help at these meals; she says it's more trouble than it's worth. I guessed what this was about. She was telling Tina Gilchrist that Adam had tried everything, and this skin condition was something permanent, so please don't mention it.

Of course, the rest of the evening was the very disaster I had predicted. Teddy was bored and kept fidgeting. At the table, he fiddled with his cell phone. Adam hardly said a word. Tina rattled on and on, in some confusion. Adam left early, saying he had to get home to his mother because she wasn't feeling well these days. He hardly tasted the food. Tina said, "Oh dear, I know I said the wrong thing. And he seemed so sensitive. I had a friend who had this awful skin rash, but my brother Jesse helped him out."

I was dead tired and frankly, was hoping she would go. Teddy was eating a second helping of dessert, a rich chocolate cake. Tina said, "Teddy, go easy on the cake, it's not good for your skin." He went right on eating: "Aw, Mom, lay off." Tina took a bowl of strawberries instead of the cake. The conversation seemed to be flagging, so, in desperation, I brought up the murder.

"Oh, such a terrible thing," Tina said. "It has everybody so upset. Did you know the police came and asked me questions? It's because of Teddy and the key."

"Yeah," Teddy said, brightly, and with great relish, "I had the key to the house. Wow—like I told Mr. May—that made me a suspect."

"Oh, go on, Teddy," she said. "Nobody thinks anything of the sort."

"*Now* they don't," he said, "Lucky me, I got an alibi. I got up about ten o'clock, and I went over to the house there, and I took a look around, watered some plants, and turned the lights off, like I was supposed to because they were coming back in the afternoon—how was I supposed to know they'd be hours and hours late, and the place would be all dark? Anyway, I went over to Omar's house, and I was there all afternoon watching sports stuff on the TV—they've got a huge flat-screen TV—and Omar's folks were there, and they brought in pizza, sausage pizza, and Buzz came over, too, and Omar's cousin came over—he's in the Marine Corps believe it or not, and he kept bragging about it; me, I'd rather die, they practically torture you during basic training, and I thought this guy was a real jerk, really full of himself—but anyway, there were all these people there, and I didn't go home before six or seven, and I got all these witnesses, so I'm in the clear. I mean, the lady was dead, like, by that time. She was probably in that place already, you know, the trunk or wherever they found her. No way I could have done it. Hey, how about you, Mom?"

"Teddy, what do you mean: what about me?"

"Hey, I mean, do you have an alibi, Mom? Like me. You could be a suspect too."

"Oh, Teddy," she said, "be serious. I know you're joking, but it's just so awful, I don't even want you to joke about it."

He ignored this reasonable request. "They ask people, don't they, like, 'Where were you? Can you prove it?' and that sort of thing. But you've got a witness, Mom, so I'm not worried."

"A witness, Teddy? What on earth are you talking about? They did ask me where I was that Sunday and if I could account for my activities. And actually, I can't. I said I was home, I was cleaning the house, I did some shopping—I can't really remember. So I suppose I don't have an alibi, but why should I need one? I never met the woman in my life."

"But you weren't alone, Mom," Teddy said. "You had company."

"What do you mean, company? You weren't there, Teddy, why should you say a thing like that? You went to Omar's house—like you said—you were there all afternoon."

"Yeah, I was. And then Buzz came over too, on his bicycle, like I said, and he goes by our house, and when he gets to Omar's house, he says, 'Hey, who was that at your house, Teddy? Who was visiting your mom? Is it a boyfriend?' And I said, 'First I've heard of it.' He said, 'Well, I saw some guy coming out of the house, young guy, and he got into a car and drove off.'"

Tina turned bright red. "He must have made a mistake," she said, "there was nobody there."

"Hey, Mom, it's okay, look, it's none of their business. I told Buzz that my mom dates sometimes—she goes on some website, and she has coffee with guys who call her up—bunch of losers usually. Nobody special. So maybe this was one of those guys. He came over, had coffee or something. Or maybe it was a salesman, who knows?"

"Oh, Teddy."

"Look, Mom, I know it wasn't a salesman. Maybe it was the one you told me about, the nice one."

"Teddy," she said, "these nice people here, they're not interested, really, I don't think it's proper to talk about these things."

"Yeah, but it's important," Teddy said. "Did you know, Mr. May here, he's not just a lawyer? He's some kind of investigator, and he's working on the case."

I had to break in, "Teddy, I'm not an investigator, and I'm not working on the case." But I saw him winking at his mother, sending her the message: "don't listen to this denial." I thought, nothing is going right this evening. Celia asked whether people wanted anything else, more coffee or tea. She was just as unhappy as I was with the evening—that was clear—since another dream of fixing up Adam had vanished in a puff of smoke. Mercifully, Tina was now as eager to go as I was to see her go. She and Teddy were soon out the door.

I thought that would be the last I'd see of her. In fact, I heard from her the very next day.

18

Indeed, Tina phoned me at my office late in morning. "Frank," she said, "may I call you that? I feel ... I need to talk to you about last night."

"Oh, Tina," I said. "There's no need to. It was," I lied, "a lovely evening, and we're so glad you could come. Celia thinks so too."

"I should talk to her. She went to so much trouble. The food was so good, it's as if she read my mind. I just adore lamb. And asparagus. And Teddy couldn't get enough of the dessert, he's got a real sweet tooth. But ... my Teddy, he's my pride and joy, but sometimes he talks too much. And now that I know you're ... well, involved in this case ..."

"No, no ..."

"I feel I owe you an explanation ..."

"Really you don't."

"I know I shouldn't ask this of you. But ... could you possibly come to my place some evening, maybe even tonight? It won't take you long. I want you to meet somebody. Please. It's important to me."

I was extremely reluctant, as you can imagine. And this was a Monday—I hate to confess it—but one of the public television stations broadcasts BBC mystery programs on Monday evenings, and I find them the perfect television junk food. I look forward to sitting in the family room after dinner, drinking my coffee and watching these shows.

"Possibly Tuesday night ..."

"Oh, God bless you, that's so kind of you."

We fixed a time: eight o'clock. Celia, when I told her what was up, expressed extreme displeasure. "Frank," she said, "as you know, I really like this woman. I know it didn't work out with Adam. He's so shy, and the poor woman, she didn't mean it, but she said exactly the wrong things. As I said, I do like her, but ten to one she wants to talk about this wretched case—and I don't want you involved, I've told you that dozens of times."

"You could be right," I said. "But maybe she has some sort of legal problem, I really think I'd better go." This was, I have to confess, somewhat disingenuous. I doubted very much that Tina Gilchrist was about to become a client of mine, or that she even had what it takes to be an important, paying client. No, for sure she wanted to talk about the case. And though I always insisted I was not involved—in the first place nobody believed me, and in the second place, I *was* inordinately intrigued with the whole affair.

I drove to the house. It was a simple, two-story tract house, but fairly pretty. It resembled Margot's house, but not so much that anybody with two eyes and a brain couldn't tell them apart. I rang the doorbell. Tina opened the door, and said, "Oh Frank, thank you for coming," then she led me into her living room. As I entered the room, I saw a young man who got up from his place on the sofa and came up to me to shake hands.

"I'm Griffin Peabody," he said. He was tall, a bit stooped, and lanky, with dirty blonde hair. I noticed his hands, which were bony and rather long, a bit like his cousin's. He was fairly good-looking, I would say, but seemed shy, and had something of an awkward smile. He was, I think, in his late 20's. He was wearing a plaid shirt, blue jeans, and running shoes. I sat down in an easy chair across from him.

"Griffin is a friend of mine," Tina said. "I know Teddy has been saying things about him. Teddy is a good boy, but sometimes he gets carried away. He gets enthusiastic about things. I wanted you to come here, so you could talk to Griffin and hear his side of the story. Meanwhile, can I get you some coffee or tea?"

I opted for coffee. Tina disappeared into the kitchen. "Griffin," I said, "really, I don't know what people have told you about me; I'm not really involved in this at all. Well, I do represent Margot Williams, and she's the one who found a dead body in her house. Anyway, about that awful event, I certainly don't think you had anything to do with it, and I know Teddy has a vivid imagination and he has this story about you possibly getting the key to the house—but I don't put any stock in that— really, I don't."

He nodded, and replied, "I'm glad you said that. I know what Teddy's been saying, and of course it's ridiculous. I didn't even know he had a key to that house. And I never met Geena King. It's not her I want to talk about, but Ramsey Hardcastle."

"Okay."

"I'm a post-doc, I have a grant, and I'm working in the psych department. I was working, in fact, with Ramsey Hardcastle. I did know Lissa, of course, from the department and ... I dated her, or tried to date her. I know, it's all coincidences. I think Tina told you how we met, how she tripped and I picked up her groceries. I should add that I also saw her at Lissa's ... I was there one day, and she came over for some neighbor-type thing. We became friends. I was attracted to Lissa; I'll be honest with you. She's a very attractive woman. But I never got anywhere with her. I'm not that great with women. Tina was ... so sympathetic. I know she's much older than I am, but does that matter?"

"No, not at all," I said, though frankly I thought it did matter.

"I was here with Tina that afternoon," he said, "on the day that woman got killed. Well, part of the time. That's not the point. The point is, I saw Teddy once or twice, for a minute, on this or that occasion—and we were frankly embarrassed, Tina and I, because, well, you know why—anyway the idea that I got the key from Teddy somehow is ridiculous, like I told you. And why would I do anything to this woman? I didn't even know her."

"Of course," I said.

"Ramsey Hardcastle," he said, "that's another story. He was a very difficult man, I think everybody admits that. And I was in a funny position because of my cousin, Philpott. I think you know about that, him and Mildred Hardcastle. She's a disturbed person, and I'm afraid she's a bad influence on my cousin. But that's not what I want to tell you. I have what I think is important information."

"Important information?"

"About Ramsey. About his death."

I should have told him, very firmly, that important information was for the police, not for Frank May, attorney-at-law. But of course I did no such thing. I'm only human.

"I should give you a little background," he said. "I did my undergraduate work at Berkeley, and that's where I got my doctorate as well. My chief adviser was Herschel Bierstube, a great guy. But I had a kind of advisory committee, and Ramsey Hardcastle was on it. Herschel was interested in sexuality and he supervised me ... I had this great project. At least I think it was great. I won't bore you with the theoretical underpinnings, but Herschel had ideas about the nature of lust, you know, sexual desire. We interviewed dozens of people about their sex lives, and the key point was to ask them, 'What color was your orgasm?' Well, that's a peculiar question, and they'd say, 'What color? What on earth do you mean?' and we'd say, 'Think about it, if you had to pick a color to describe your last orgasm, would it be red, yellow, pink, orange, purple or whatever?' And then the follow up, 'Next time you have an orgasm, is it the same color?' I won't bore you with details ... we got some great data and I got my doctorate, and then I got a post-doc and a grant from the National Science Foundation. I came to Stanford because, well, Ramsey Hardcastle was just about tops in the field, and it was a great privilege—I thought—to get to work with him. What I didn't realize was what a bastard he was: cruel, selfish, arrogant, domineering, manipulative. But he was some kind of genius too. Nobody knew so much about the way the mind works, at least as far as anger is concerned, or sexual desire—and how the two are related.

"Anyway, about a week before he died, I think it was about a week, I'm not really clear on the date, Ramsey called me into his office, and he said, 'I have something I want you to do for me. But it has to be kept absolutely quiet. I want to trust you, and I do trust you. You've got to swear to absolute secrecy. It's about a piece of research, but I can't tell you any more about it, not now. Do I have your promise—not to say a word to anybody?' Well, of course, I said, 'Sure.' I made the promise. Naturally, I thought this was peculiar; but he was the boss, so I agreed. 'Okay,' he said, 'here's the first thing. I'm going to give you two names, and I want you to find out all you can about these two people. Discreetly. Later on, I'll tell you why I want this done. Meanwhile, it has to be kept absolutely secret—I can't stress that enough. Above all, do not tell your cousin Philpott.'

"That did make the situation a bit awkward, because of the family thing—I used to be close to my cousin, but the relationship had become, well, strained. I promised to keep this very quiet. He said, 'The first name, it's a man. His name is Laszlo Szekely.' He had to spell it for me. Hungarian name. Ramsey said, 'This man is a musician, a violinist. I want you to find out everything you can about this guy. His address, his whereabouts, what he's like, anything you can find out. But like I told you: discreetly.' Well, I did that. It wasn't hard to find stuff about him. He was quite well known, he's a pretty prominent musician, and he had an entry in Wikipedia, and so on. He normally lives in London; he's married to an American woman named Edith. They don't have children, apparently. He used to play with an orchestra in London called St. Martin in the Fields. But he left and he does chamber music now. He's the second violinist in a string quartet—the Farkas Quartet—they're the quartet in residence at some university, I forget which one, maybe it's Vanderbilt, but they travel around a lot, giving concerts in various places."

"And he never told you why he was interested in this particular guy? Did he know him? What was the story?"

"Honestly, I have no idea. The man has been in this area, I know that. The quartet gave a concert at Stanford, recently, at the Bing Auditorium. Oh, there was lots of stuff about Szekely, on the web. Mostly about his career, his concerts, who he studied with, that sort of thing. There were two items in British newspapers, about this guy—I mean, aside from all those concert reviews, and so on. One was a long story in a London Sunday paper, a sort of interview with him. I printed it out to show Ramsey. Kind of interesting. It told about his life. He was born in Budapest, his father was a singer and his mother some sort of political activist; his family got in trouble with the Hungarian government, when Hungary was still a communist country. I guess the father went to jail, and I think he died there. Somehow, the family got to England—they had a relative there—Szekely was a young boy at the time. They were very poor, but somebody recognized that the boy had talent, and helped him study music. At one time, he was just scraping by, making a living strolling around in a Hungarian restaurant playing gypsy music and collecting tips. Meanwhile, he was studying at the Royal Academy. After that, of course, he got an orchestra job and then, later, he went with this quartet.

"The other item was even more interesting. It was in all the papers, but just a paragraph, except in the tabloids. In one of the tabloids, the headline was 'Dis-chord in North London: Violinist Accused of Domestic Violence.' According to the paper, somebody called the police to his place—he lived in an apartment building in north Finchley—and the neighbors said there was a huge ruckus in his apartment, loud noises, people screaming, and it wasn't the first time, etc. Well, the wife, Edith, complained to the police when they got there. She said Laszlo had gotten drunk and violent, he was beating her, and she wanted him arrested. She said he was a maniac, a monster; and Laszlo, he said, 'She's a damn liar.' He denied everything— said he wasn't drunk, never drank, and that actually it was Edith who was the monster, that she'd hit him over the head with a frying pan and cursed him. "'She is a real devil,' he was quoted as saying, 'She threatened to kill me, smash my violins ... the woman is crazy, she should be locked up.' And in the end, I guess, everybody calmed down—the police didn't arrest anybody, and just went away. The paper made all kinds of caustic comments, 'This violinist's life is lacking in harmony,' and so on ... That's all there was. No idea what happened later, whether they're still together, or what. Sounds like they were headed toward the divorce court. That was all I could find out about him personally."

"You said he did a concert around here, at Stanford."

"Yeah. As I said, the Farkas Quartet is pretty well known. Especially for brand new music, avant-garde stuff. Not my taste. I mean, they play the classics, but they also do some far-out pieces. At their Stanford concert, they played a piece by a local composer, somebody named Milo Feigenblatt."

That caught my attention. I knew Milo Feigenblatt; he lived in the Bay area, and indeed wrote pretty far-out music, including that really weird piece called, "Concerto for Dentist and Orchestra." He was involved in another of those strange affairs that seem to haunt me—my dentist's receptionist had been found dead, killed in the dentist's office. Milo was another patient of the dentist, and had been scheduled to see him that day. That's when we met, but that's another story.

"And you don't know if Hardcastle was there? In the audience?"

"No I don't. But I was interested in reading about this concert," Griffin said, "because it seemed to be the only possible connection between Ramsey Hardcastle and this Hungarian violinist. I have no idea whether Ramsey was a music-lover, whether he went to this concert, or whatever. There was a pretty extensive review of the concert in the *San Francisco Chronicle*. Mostly because of the Feigenblatt piece, which was sandwiched in between a Haydn quartet and something by Brahms. For Milo's piece, the musicians took off all their clothes—right there in the auditorium—all except their underwear. They were wearing white boxer shorts. Then they pretended to be playing, but actually they were just acting, and no music came out. After a few minutes of this—and I imagine the audience must have been a bit restless—a recording started playing marches by Sousa. Then they got dressed again, and played what sounded like cats yowling—I'm quoting the reviewer. And apparently the composer was there, in the audience, and he took a bow and made a little talk about how he was trying to strip classical music of its stuffiness, and reduce it to its essence, 'take off the fancy clothing, get down to the underwear level,' and he also wanted to explore the relationship between music and noise, and that sort of thing. Anyway, the reviewer for the Chronicle hated it."

"And did you report this stuff to Professor Hardcastle?"

"I sent him an email. I scanned the newspaper articles, and the concert review, and I attached them to the email. No reaction. As to why he wanted to know, I don't have a clue. He didn't tell me. Not at that time, anyway. Then he got killed—and I have to wonder—is this Szekely guy somehow involved? Ordinarily, I would have thought, no, it has nothing to do with his death, it's maybe something about his research, or something else ... except that, well, remember, I said he was going to give me two names. Szekely was the first. The real surprise was the second name."

"The second name?"

"The second name was Margot Williams. He said, 'This one, it's different because I know who she is. Did you read in the paper about some people finding a dead body in a house? That's the woman. Her house. Her name is Margot Williams.' But of course I knew already who she was, because I was friends with Tina Gilchrist, and I knew that Margot was some kind of neighbor and that when she went away Teddy watered the plants and that sort of thing—and he had the key to the house. As you can imagine, Tina and I talked a lot about that awful business—it was pretty shocking, after all—and the police had come to the house and talked to her, and to Teddy, so it was something pretty much in our minds."

"Okay, but why was Ramsey Hardcastle interested? I know that the dead woman was the sister of his secretary, but still, it seems odd. What was the connection to Margot Williams? I assume you have no idea."

"No, no idea. He didn't tell me a thing. Not then. He was, well, sort of mysterious. But he seemed agitated. Maybe more agitated about the Hungarian guy than about Margot Williams; I really don't know. He said he'd explain it to me, in the end. I said, 'Well, what is it you want to know about Margot Williams?' But just then, the chair of the department poked her head in the door, and said, 'Ramsey, we're waiting for you;'

there was some sort of meeting, faculty meeting. And he said he had to go and he'd tell me all about this later on. And he said, 'Don't mention this conversation to anybody, do you hear?' He kept repeating that. I promised. He said, 'Griffin, I'm serious: absolute silence. If you handle this right, I'll make it worth your while.'"

"What did he mean by that? Worth your while? How? Money?"

"Oh, no. Something more important. He said, 'I'm an important person in my field; I can make you or break you, Griffin. You're not a damn fool like your cousin. If you do what I want, I'll see to it that you get ahead; I've got influence, I can get you a job at a top school.'"

"But you never found out why he mentioned those names."

"No. Like I told you. He was busy, I guess, and then—well, then he was dead. Do you think these names had ... something to do with it? With his death?

"I have no idea, Griffin."

Yet there had to be some connection. I couldn't for the life of me imagine why Ramsey Hardcastle would mention Margot's name. She swore she knew nothing about the dead woman. Or about Ramsey Hardcastle. Was she lying?

And this Hungarian violinist? What on earth was that all about? I mulled it over, while eating cake and drinking coffee. "Maybe this Hungarian dude killed Ramsey Hardcastle," Griffin said. "Maybe he hired a hit man, or did it himself. I'm trying to find out where he was, and when, the day Ramsey died. He could be the guy."

I had trouble envisioning this Hungarian plot, or what it had to do with Ramsey Hardcastle. A homicidal second violinist? Maybe Ramsey hated classical music. Or maybe, instead, he loved it, and he went to the concert, heard Milo's music—if you can call it music—and it drove him crazy; I'm sure it would drive *me* crazy.

"It's far-fetched," Griffin said. "But I prefer it to some of the other theories about who killed Ramsey."

"Other theories? Like what?"

"I don't mean my cousin Philpott. I know him; he just

couldn't do something like this. He couldn't kill anybody. He's really weak, harmless, you know what I mean? I've known him all my life. He used to be really scared of spiders. Anyway, that was a long time ago. Now he's hooked up with this awful woman, Mildred, Ramsey's wife. She's really bad, well, maybe not bad, more like crazy. He's infatuated with her, God knows why. I tried to talk him out of it ... I said, 'Phil, this is no good, you've got to break off from her. She's poison.' But he refused to listen."

"And you think *she* did it? Mildred Hardcastle?"

"I think she did. I mean, who else? I think she killed that poor woman, and maybe it was some kind of insane jealousy. She's full of rage and anger. Funny thing: that was Ramsey's field, rage and anger. And lust. Mildred was so worked up about all the evil deeds he did, or she said he did, that I think she killed that woman, and then got rid of the professor too. It's the only thing that makes sense."

"You're talking about Geena? The woman whose body was in Margot Williams' house? You think Mildred Hardcastle killed her?"

"Who knows? Somebody did. And she's crazy enough to do it."

I couldn't resist the temptation to ask him a question: "That was a Sunday, right? And you were at the Gilchrist house, weren't you?"

I'm not very subtle, I guess. Griffin gave me a look. It was plain what the look meant: You're asking me if I have an alibi? You really think I might be involved?

"At the house?" he said, "Actually, I wasn't. I stayed overnight, yes. Tina and I went to a movie at the multiplex, and then we had coffee, and talked and talked. We were in Redwood City, downtown. I guess we came back to her house around midnight, and ... I was tired. She asked me in, and I spent the night in a guest room. I got up real early the next morning and I left. I didn't want Teddy to see me, didn't want him to know, well, that I stayed in the house all night. I went home, took a shower, got dressed—and then I went to see my cousin ... But he wasn't home; I don't know where he was. With

Mildred, probably. I went back to Tina's house—I knew Teddy wasn't home, we had a spot of lunch—but I didn't stay terribly long. I guess Teddy's friend saw me leaving the house. I went home, did some work on the computer. I heard about the killing the next day. It got me scared."

"Scared? Why?"

"Because ... that woman, she's so crazy, and ... I didn't want her to drag my cousin into this thing. Tina had talked to me about the first murder, the body in the house, and how Teddy had been watering the plants and had the key, and so on, and later, she told me how Teddy had thought at first that the dead woman was Lissa, and how Lissa had walked in on him. When I heard all of this, a bell rang. I thought—it had to be Mildred Hardcastle! Tina and I, lately, we've been talking about this a lot. Tina asked me, 'Is it possible that Phil did it, that she made him do it somehow?' I know he's weak, I know she bosses him around, but still, I said, 'No he's not that kind of a person, he couldn't kill a fly. I'm sure of that.' That's what I told her and that's what I'm telling you, too. Really. It can't be him."

"If you say so, Griffin. After all, you know him; I really don't."

"I'm sure I'm right."

"You know, Tina lied. She said she was alone that Sunday afternoon."

"Maybe to protect me. Or she was thinking of Teddy—Teddy means everything to her. She doesn't want him to think that there's uh, more to our friendship than ... well, just friendship."

Griffin, like everybody else, seemed firmly convinced I was some sort of secret operative or master sleuth. I've given up trying to argue against this insane idea. People read mystery stories, and they're used to the idea of Miss Marple, or Father Brown, or Nero Wolfe, or any other member of that motley crew. In mystery novels, these amateur detectives come from every walk of life, a rabbi, a stockbroker, a cowboy, God knows what else, even cats and dogs. Next, somebody will write a series of mysteries about a prostitute who solves mysteries—

maybe it's been done already—so why not a nerdish suburban lawyer?

At least he didn't ask me what color my orgasm was. I do have orgasms, but they, and their color, are absolutely nobody's business.

19

Had I learned much from my talk with Griffin Peabody? As far as the murder of Geena King was concerned, neither he nor Tina Gilchrist had a real alibi. But did they need one? There was absolutely no reason to think either of them had any reason to kill Geena King. Had either of them even met her?

And I hadn't had the nerve to ask whether they had an alibi for the night Ramsey Hardcastle was strangled. At least there I could imagine some sort of motive. Maybe. At least for Griffin. But, in fact, when I thought about it, what did he have to gain from killing Ramsey Hardcastle? Nothing. In fact, the opposite: unlike his cousin, he hadn't quarreled with Ramsey. Ramsey seemed to have confidence in him; and now that Hardcastle was dead, who could advance Griffin's career?

And then there was the mysterious business of the Hungarian violinist. That was something relevant, I suppose. But what? In bed that night, I had trouble sleeping. I kept turning things over and over in my mind. Who *was* this Hungarian, and why was Ramsey so interested in him?

Maybe it had nothing at all to do with Ramsey's death. Maybe it was something altogether different. I had this fantasy though: this violinist, Szekely, he's a passionate, violent man. Let's say he plays like a fury, attacking the violin with raw, almost indecent emotion, and he has a secret—he's a serial killer, a man with an insane urge to kill—and his job is a perfect cover. He's a member of a string quartet. They do a concert here, a concert there, stay one or two nights in a city, and then move on. They finish playing at night and then he leaves the other members of the quartet to prowl the streets. Who would suspect that this man, this concert violinist, is a madman, leaving behind a trail of bodies? A musical Jack the Ripper.

Maybe it's only certain music that touches off this madness. He's like a werewolf, only it's not the full moon that does it, but something else. Maybe a certain key, B-flat, let's say. Maybe it's the music of Milo Feigenblatt. Anyway, he meets Geena King—in a bar, say—and he strangles her. Then, cackling madly, he plays the violin over her corpse. He deposits her body in the house of Margot Williams. Somehow, Ramsey Hardcastle finds out about this, or at least he gets suspicious—but that suspicion is Ramsey's death sentence.

I know this is crazy.

How would Ramsey find out? And why? And how did Laszlo get the body into the Williams house? And why that house?

Finally, I drifted off to sleep.

* * *

Even in the cool light of day, I liked the Laszlo Szekely idea. I don't like suspecting people I know personally. I had never met this Hungarian violinist. I didn't even know what he looked like. When I tried to conjure up his image, I saw him as something like Bela Lugosi in Dracula, a sinister figure in a black cape. Of course that part was nonsense. But it was nonetheless tempting to put the blame on the violinist from Hungary.

We don't normally connect classical music with murder. Some of the more far-out, hideous rock-and-roll music, yes. But Bach and Beethoven no; and surely not Mozart. I do remember a horror movie I once saw, it was called something like *The Beast with Five Fingers*. The main character, if you could call it that, was a murderous severed hand that loved to choke people to death and, when it wasn't killing people, it played the piano—a piano version of Bach's *Chaconne in D Minor*, to be exact.

Of course, all of this speculation was totally ridiculous. Moreover, as Celia never ceased to remind me, all of it was also none of my business.

Still, I had this constant, nagging curiosity, like an itch on a guy's back that can't be scratched because he can't reach it. There was no reason why I shouldn't or couldn't ask a few harmless questions, was there?

I called Margot Williams, who was, after all, my client, and I asked her how she was doing, how things were going. Not well, she told me, and she added, "if only they would solve this thing, oh, Frank, I'd give anything to know that it's all over and I could go back to a normal life. You know I'm pregnant; I keep wondering if all this worry is bad for the baby. Dr. Pillbrow, she's my obstetrician, she tells me everything is OK, but I can't help wondering."

"Margot, can I ask you something?"

"Of course, Frank, what is it?"

"Does the name Laszlo Szekely mean anything to you?"

"Who?" I had to spell the name for her. I explained he was a Hungarian violinist.

"What's this about, Frank? I absolutely never heard of this man. A violinist? From Hungary?"

"Well, somehow Ramsey Hardcastle knew about him ... He plays with a string quartet. They did a concert at Stanford. You didn't happen to go? Or Jim, did he go?"

"Oh, I never go to those concerts. I suppose I should, but really, I don't know much about classical music. I took piano lessons for a year, but I never practiced and I was hopeless. So I gave it up. And Jim is practically tone deaf. Our tastes in music are pretty ordinary. But I'll ask him, if he ever heard of this guy."

"Do that, Margot. And call me back."

Jim—she told me when she called back the next day—was also clueless. The name meant nothing to him. "Like I told you, he never goes to these concert things. We're just not musical. Anyway, how would we know such a man? But, Frank, why are you asking? Is he the killer? Is he a suspect? Did you get this information from the police? You're giving me hope. God bless you."

I didn't have the heart to tell her I was just as baffled as she was. And the police, I am sure, were not exactly hot on the trail of Laszlo Szekely, the mad violinist. They did not even know he existed. Griffin had never mentioned his name to the police—indeed, the police had never talked to Griffin at all—and he was happy to keep things that way.

20

I hate keeping secrets from my wife. And I usually don't. Certainly not big secrets. Small, tiny, harmless secrets: that's another story. Like what I had for lunch, and whether I ate snacks at work during the day.

I guess this particular secret is sort of in the middle. It relates to the body in Margot's house, and the death of Ramsey Hardcastle. And the secret is that I am obsessing over this affair.

It was evening. Celia was patiently and calmly knitting. I sat near her in the living room. The television set was off, as often happens, since there was absolutely nothing we wanted to see. I sat there with a book in my hand. But I wasn't reading. I was thinking. About the case. I suppose if that's all that my secret consisted of—thinking about the case—Celia really couldn't, in good conscience, object too much. But there was more. There was the temptation, which I found irresistible, to do at least a teeny-weeny bit of investigation. I denied to one and all that I had such a role and, in truth, it's not as if anybody had hired me to investigate. Still, I was more active than I liked to admit.

Right now, I was thinking up an excuse to talk to Lissa King. She had been Ramsey Hardcastle's secretary. Some secretaries know all there is to know about their bosses, their business and professional affairs. Surely she would know something about the Hungarian violinist. I wracked my brains for an excuse, but I couldn't come up with a good one. In desperation, I turned to Teddy. I sent him a text message. This, of course, is the chosen method of communication with the young, as I know from my daughters. They never answer their phones, but they do respond to texts. I assumed Teddy was the same and I asked him to ride his bike to my office the next day, "but only after class, OK? There's something I need you to do."

Teddy showed up, as I knew he would. I told him he could help me out.

I could see eagerness written all over his face. "Sure thing, Mr. May."

"I'm not really working on the case, you know that, Teddy? Still, I'm interested and Margot is my client after all—and if I could help her out, it'd be terrific. And you could give me a hand."

He nodded his head. I said, "I heard something—never mind from who—and it's really important. I need you to check up on, uh, a certain person."

"Wow, Mr. May," he said. "Awesome."

I told him that I had a source (I didn't say who) who had revealed the name of somebody who might have been threatening Ramsey Hardcastle, and who maybe had something to do with Geena King (I simply made this up), so I needed to talk to Lissa King.

"Teddy, you know her, you do things for her when she goes away. I thought maybe, somehow, you could help me with this."

"Wow. Sure thing. I'll tell her, you've got a big clue, she should talk to you, okay?"

"Well, no, not exactly, Teddy, forget the clue; just say I need to talk to her, confidentially ... Have you seen her recently?"

"Yeah, I did some stuff for her around the house. Mr. May, I feel sorry for her. She's a major mess, she really is. I mean, okay, her sister's dead, and the guy she worked for too, that would freak anybody out—but she seemed, well, scared."

"Scared?"

"Yeah, scared. Like somebody was threatening her—and she hasn't been going to work. I asked her about that, if she lost her job now that the guy is dead, and she said, 'It's not that. They want me to stay on, for a while anyway,' but she hasn't gone in. She tells them she's sick, and she just stays home and locks the door, so I have to ring the bell, and she says, 'Who's there?' and when I say 'Teddy,' she opens up. She's sitting there in the dark, and I said to her, 'Miss King, really, you can't be like this, you got to get out, you know, fresh air.' But she says, 'I don't feel well,' and, man, she did look funny, you know, dark circles under her eyes, hair a mess—not like she was really sick, you know, sneezing or a fever or whatever—and she says, 'Teddy, I'll give you money and a list of stuff and can you get me food at Safeway so I don't have to go out until I feel better. I'll pay you.' And I said, 'Look, something's bothering you, you're scared of something, maybe the police can help you,' and she said, 'No, no, no, I can't do that.'"

"Teddy," I said, "she won't see the police, but do you think she would see *me*? Could you make up some story?" I was almost ashamed of myself. I knew that there was basically only one story that would work: Frank May, the great detective, was busy working on the case.

Teddy was only too glad to help me. Maybe he was a little disappointed—maybe he thought I had some real detective work for him to do—but he didn't complain, he did his job, and Lissa said yes. The next afternoon, I drove over to Lissa's house, canceling an appointment with a client, which shows you how low I had sunk. I parked the car, and rang the doorbell. It took a while, but I heard a voice: "Who's there?" and I identified myself, and she looked through a little peephole in the door, and finally opened it.

The house was fairly dark; the shades were drawn. A dim table-lamp was on in the living room. Lissa looked pale—frightened, I guess. Or was I reading things into her face?

"I'm so glad you could come. Teddy said maybe you could help me."

"Lissa," I said, "I'd love to help you. But help you with what? Is something the matter?"

She burst into tears. "It's ... this whole awful thing. I can't eat, I can't sleep. My poor sister. Dead. Murdered. And then my boss. I keep wondering: who's next? Is it me?"

I told her her reaction was understandable, even normal. All of these events, they must be totally traumatic. And she was, in a way, at the center of it. "But why," I asked, "should you think you're in some sort of danger?"

She just shook her head, cried some more, and said nothing. I sat quietly waiting. Then she said, "Frank, if only ... if only you could help me. They say you have a skill ..."

"Honestly, Lissa, I can't claim I do. I would help you, if I could, but don't expect me to do detective work."

"You talk to people. You know things. They tell you things," she said.

I saw an opening. "Some people do. Not you, though."

"I don't have anything to tell. My sister ... I told you, she was so private. I don't really know much about her life. Or why anybody would want to kill her. Did you know she was pregnant?"

"I heard that, yes. Did *you* know?"

"Absolutely not."

"And ... do you know who the father was? Could it possibly be ... Ramsey Hardcastle?"

"He never met my sister. Never. He wouldn't ... do a thing like that."

"Lissa," I said, "I have to ask you a painful question. Was there anything between *you* and Ramsey Hardcastle?"

"Nothing!" she said, raising her voice. "He was an awful man, terrible, but he didn't do that sort of thing. Not with me. I know that crazy woman says things, she spreads rumors, but it is absolutely nuts, and, like I said, there's no truth to it. Nothing at all."

"Did you ever hear of a man named Laszlo Szekely? A violinist?"

"Never," she said. There was a slight, momentary hesitation—just a second or two, but I noticed it. Was she lying?

"Did Ramsey go to concerts? On campus?"

"I don't think so. I really don't know. Honestly. I was his secretary, assistant, whatever. I didn't know much about his personal life, really."

"He had a lot of enemies, didn't he? People in the department, that sort of thing."

"Yes. Absolutely. People in the department, they hated him."

"Did he have other enemies?"

"Frank, how would I know? I told you, I was just the woman in his office. I was a piece of furniture, really."

"Lissa," I said, "you're not telling the whole story. You're scared. Of what? Why do you feel you're in danger?"

She looked me straight in the eye. I felt she was about to say something. But then she didn't. It was as if there was a closed door somewhere, a door to a room, and I was not invited in. It was obvious she knew more than she was telling me, but it was hopeless to try to get it out of her. At least at that stage.

Shortly afterwards, I left. At the time, I felt the visit was a failure. But apparently, I had laid the groundwork for something. What it was would appear quite soon.

* * *

I drove home, parked the car, and went for a short walk. It was a clear, bright, moonlit night; the temperature was mild, a bit bracing maybe, but perfect walking weather. Somehow I felt I needed to clear my head.

Two people dead. Connected, but only in the most tangential way. Geena King was the sister of Ramsey Hardcastle's assistant, Lissa. But apparently they had never met. If you believed what people said. There were other connections, even more tangential. Griffin Peabody was the cousin of Philpott Peabody, who had been victimized by Ramsey Hardcastle, and Griffin was a friend of Tina Gilchrist, whose boy, Teddy, had the key to Margot Williams' house. And Margot had never met (she said) Ramsey Hardcastle, but he mentioned her name to Griffin. Add to the list the name of a Hungarian violinist, Laszlo Szekely, who played with the Farkas Quartet. The violinist: that was perhaps the strangest thing of all. Nobody seemed to know him or anything about him. Then there was Ramsey Hardcastle's strange and mysterious will, which Sylvan had told me about.

And the key to Margot's house ... the key Teddy wore around his neck. Was it possible that his mother made a copy and gave it to somebody? If so, why?

I woke up in the middle of the night, after a vivid and frightening nightmare. All the talk about the Hungarian violinist had muddled up my poor unconscious brain. In my dream, I was at a concert—a chamber-music concert. A string quartet was playing. All four of the musicians were wearing black capes, and they *all* looked like Bela Lugosi, in his signature role of Dracula, the vampire from Transylvania. As I got up from my seat and walked toward the players, they turned toward me and I saw their scowling faces, their long, sharp teeth, and the blood of innocent people dripping down their chins. Who are you? I asked. All four of them were the same person, and they whispered, in unison, the dreaded name: *I am Laszlo Szekely, the vampire.*

Fortunately, at that point I woke up.

21

A few days went by. I felt I was making little or no progress. But of course, as I told myself, I wasn't supposed to be making progress. Progress was not my job. I was busy with clients, anyway. And with my normal life. Celia hatched her latest scheme to find a woman for Adam Finkel—this time, a divorced woman from her book club, a woman in her 40's who told Celia she was "on the prowl for a man." I told Celia not to bother.

"Nobody who's on the prowl for a man is prowling for Adam Finkel. Believe me." But Celia never gives up.

"I told her," she said, "that I knew this man, lovely man, a math teacher and she said she's always been good at math. And her last husband was an engineer." Clearly, this was another lost cause, but I shrugged my shoulders and let it happen.

Then, about a week later, the case re-entered my life, somewhat dramatically. I had a telephone call from Philpott Peabody, asking if he could come to see me. He said, "I have something to say to you. Privately." Of course I said yes. We fixed on a time.

Now he was there, sitting across from me in my office. I couldn't help thinking what a miserable specimen of humanity he was, at least on the surface. Scrawny, with bloodshot eyes. He was wearing a white dress-shirt, but I could see that the collar was frayed and he hadn't bothered to button the collar buttons. He was wearing ugly shoes, and he needed a shave. And I noticed again his prominent Adam's apple, his sallow complexion, his receding chin.

"You're wondering why I'm here," he said.

"Well, actually, yes," I said.

"I know you met my cousin Griffin," he said. "You had a talk with him. And I know you've been hired to investigate this case."

"I did meet your cousin, yes. And I did talk to him. That part is true. But nobody hired me to investigate this case. Nobody."

"I've heard otherwise," he said.

I denied it again, but like everybody else, he ignored my denial. "Griffin has been telling you stories," he said. "And I want to clear things up. He's been telling you things about me, and about Mildred; maybe he's trying to connect us with ... with Professor Hardcastle's death. But I want to tell you what actually happened the night he died. Griffin just doesn't know anything about this. Nothing at all. And I don't think he's somebody you should trust."

"Why not?"

"He's on the other side. I mean, he was a creature of Ramsey Hardcastle, an acolyte; he was under that man's spell. His whole career depended on Hardcastle—Griffin's career was going nowhere, believe me. The work he was doing was worthless. All this stuff about the psychology of the orgasm, the way he was approaching it, I tell you, it was no good, it was terrible work, and the statistics were bad; and anyway, if anything came of it, Ramsey Hardcastle would simply steal it, publish under his own name, and Griffin would be lucky if he got so much as a footnote. That man would throw Griffin to the wolves, believe me. I warned Griffin, I told him, I said, 'The man is a monster,' but he paid no attention to me.

"And I know that Griffin thinks ... bad thoughts about Mildred. He doesn't know Mildred. Griffin doesn't know women at all. He's counting orgasms, what's that all about? He thinks orgasms have colors, but they don't. Anyway, that doesn't matter.

"That night, the night Ramsey died, Mildred and I were on campus. We didn't know Ramsey would be in his office. Frankly, we were going to break in. Well, not exactly break in— Mildred still had a key and I had one too—we were going to go into his office that night because we were sure he was cheating and falsifying data. The man was a criminal, an academic criminal, he had no real data, he was making it up, and the proof, it would be there right in his office—and if we found the proof, we could expose him, expose him for the fake and the cheat that he is, show him up, as a charlatan, a plagiarist, a scientific fraud. We would put an end to his miserable reign of terror. We went together. Mildred, she's not a psychologist, but she wanted me there because I would be able to deal with the data, and ... well, that was the plan."

"Phil," I said, "if I can call you that, do you realize what you're saying? You and Mrs. Hardcastle, you were going to go into somebody's office, you were going to commit a crime? Why are you telling me this?"

"Do you think I don't know that this was, well, risky?" he said. "I'll be honest with you, I was scared to death. I was shaking like a leaf. But Mildred, she gave me courage. You don't know Mildred. She's awesome. She's a powerful woman. I love her, I really do. I never had a mother. My mother died when I was six. I had a stepmother, but she never showed me any affection. Mildred came into my life, and she ... she made me feel like a person again. She gave me support, real support. I don't mean to say she's a mother substitute. Well, maybe she is, but she's more than that. She gave my life meaning. She's strong, and I'm weak. I say to her, 'Mildred, why do you put up with me? I'm such a worm, an unworthy person, and you, you're so strong, so powerful.' And she is. She's got force, and character—she gets things done. Me, I'm the opposite. People always made fun of me in high school. They laughed at me. I was the skinny runt. I was bad at sports. I had pimples. Until I met Mildred, I never knew about the power of love. Don't laugh. And I don't mean sexual love. I mean just plain love."

Personally, I never doubted the power of love. What I couldn't help doubting was the power of the love emanating from this woman in her sixties, overweight, with a strident voice, hair all askew, somewhat bowlegged, who looked as if she badly needed a shower and a hair wash. Not to mention a total makeover in the wardrobe department and a personality I found repellent and that—unless I'm badly mistaken—most other people would find repellent too. A woman on the border-line of sanity. But, then again, Philpott Peabody was repellent in his own, much quieter way.

I know, I know: you can't judge a book by its cover. Was I being unfair? But it wasn't just the cover; it was what seemed to be inside the book. Maybe I'm just small-minded. Maybe I had Philpott and Mildred all wrong. Maybe I was overlooking their rich inner life. Or the power of their relationship. Maybe what they had even included "sexual love," despite what Philpott had just said. Great love doesn't depend on beauty, does it? And this business of "sexual love," including orgasms (in many colors), well, yes, there are movie stars and top models, and high school football stars—we know about *them*—but are they the only ones? I hope not.

"I know you're suspicious of the two of us," he said. "Because of Griffin, maybe. You think we killed Ramsey Hard-castle ..."

"No, no ..."

"Please, don't deny it. I have my sources. If not you, then other people think so. They know we were around there that night. People saw us on campus, outside the building. They might think we went into the building, up to his office, and that we found him there and some sort of fight took place before he ended up dead. Oh, I admit, Mildred could do that—if she wanted to. She could do anything, I never met such a powerful woman, she's a force of nature, yes, she could have killed that man, and maybe she even wanted to—the world is better off without him, and I never wanted to go to his office, I said to her, 'Mildred, let's not go there'—but she didn't kill him, I swear it, I was with her the whole time, she wasn't out of my sight. And we didn't actually do what we set out to do. Yes, we had keys to the building. And we did go inside. We took the elevator to the third floor—that's where his office was. At night, there's nobody there. People come and empty the wastebaskets, but we know their schedule, and we know when they finish. We thought: there'll be nobody there. We came with a flashlight. But when we got near his room, we saw the light was on. He was in there. And he wasn't alone, there was somebody with him."

"Somebody was with him? Do you know who that was?"

"No, we don't. Now I wish we did, I wish we had stayed around, listened in ..."

"Was it a man or a woman?"

"Honestly, I don't know. We only heard *his* voice, Ramsey Hardcastle's voice. He was quite angry about something, but we couldn't make out what he was saying and I said, 'Mildred, we can't stay here,' and she agreed, we couldn't do what we wanted to do, and so we left, quietly. We got out of there. Mildred said, 'Tomorrow, we'll come back tomorrow,' but of course we didn't come back—because by then he was already dead."

I was intrigued. "You say you don't know who it was. The person in the room."

"No. But if I had to guess, I think it was that woman. Lissa. I think she killed him. Lover's quarrel. I know her because I was in that department. She's tough, she's got a temper, and she lorded it all over us, you know, because she was the assistant to the great man himself—and, of course I think she had her hooks in him. They were lovers, I'm sure of it. I think that's why she hated Mildred so much."

"But this is just a guess, Phil—you really don't know."

"Who else could it be? He probably was dumping her. Maybe going after her sister. Maybe he killed her sister, I always wondered about that. Maybe Lissa knew this, and she wanted revenge. She was there that night, she's admitted it. And we saw her—we saw her there. She came out of the building and Mildred, well, Mildred had words with her. I tell you, she must be the one."

"You think she killed him? Look, Phil, he was strangled. I mean, she's a woman, I don't want to sound sexist—but he was, well, tall, and he looked muscular—how could she do it?"

"Oh, don't let looks fool you, Frank. That Lissa, she's young, and strong. She does exercises, yoga, that sort of thing. And don't forget—he wasn't a young man, he was in his 60's— maybe he had heart trouble or some other condition, I just don't know. I think maybe she hit him over the head, got him dazed, and then she strangled him. They found her scarf there. I know all about this."

"But, okay, suppose she did it. Why would she leave the scarf there? If she strangled him with the scarf, why didn't she grab it and run away?"

"Who knows? People panic. She saw what she did, and she freaked out. Just got out of there as fast as she could. She couldn't face it. I mean, I understand. People panic, they're cowards. Like, the other day I was in a parking garage, and I backed out—tried to back out—and I scraped the car next to me. Made a big dent. I should have left a note, I should have done something, at least taken down the license number. But I'm a coward, and I was in a panic, and I just drove off. I was sweating, I was so nervous ... and, there was another time ..."

But I interrupted this chain of minor confessions; I was not interested in Philpott's adventures in a parking garage. I had to ask the question that was on my mind.

"Phil," I said, "you worked for the man, you knew about his research. Does the name Laszlo Szekely mean anything to you?"

"Who? Can you spell that?"

I spelled it for him. "It's a Hungarian name. Do you recognize it?"

He shook his head. "Is that some psychologist? There are a lot of Hungarians in the field. Ramsey went to an international meeting once, in Budapest. Maybe this man was on the program, is that a possibility? Ramsey knew everyone in the field. Why are you asking? Who is this man?"

"He's not a psychologist. He's a violinist. Did Ramsey Hardcastle go to concerts? Chamber music concerts?"

"Maybe. I don't know."

"The professor mentioned the name to your cousin Griffin. He told Griffin to investigate the man, and he said he wanted to find out all about him. He also mentioned Margot Williams— you know, Geena King's body was found in her house. So there seems to be something there, something connected to these awful events."

"I never heard the name before. Never. A violinist? How

could that be relevant? I just don't understand."

Neither did I. Of all the mysterious aspects of this whole affair, this was perhaps the most puzzling: the Hungarian violinist. Maybe there was some simple explanation. Maybe Laszlo's hobby was psychology research and he wrote to Ramsey Hardcastle asking for a reprint of some article. Maybe Ramsey had become a fan of chamber music, and somehow Szekely's playing intrigued him—maybe he owned recordings of the Farkas Quartet. But in my heart of hearts I didn't believe any of this.

After this, Philpott Peabody had nothing particular to tell me. He left soon afterwards, having made his pitch. It was irritating that people thought I was some sort of investigator, whether official or unofficial, but it had an effect I secretly liked: it gave them an incentive to come to me and tell me what they thought, or, rather, what they wanted *me* to think.

Not that I had to believe every word they said. Was Philpott telling me the truth? He could be lying, of course, to protect his beloved Mildred. If you believed him, they both had alibis. Or rather, they were giving alibis to each other. But those alibis were worthless. They could be involved in the murder, both of them—most likely Mildred was pulling the strings, but he could be at least some sort of dithering, pathetic accomplice.

He came to see me in order to put the blame on Lissa. Maybe she did do yoga, or lift weights, or run marathons or whatever; I still had trouble picturing her strangling her boss. And Mildred—even Philpott said so—was capable of murder.

Was I getting anywhere? Not really, I suppose. The mystery fascinated me, I have to admit. I couldn't help myself, I was like an alcoholic addicted to the case. In between clients, whenever I had a spare moment, I found myself fantasizing, thinking about those two mysterious deaths. Especially the death of Ramsey Hardcastle, the great professor killed in his office in the psychology building at Stanford University; right on the hallowed grounds of the old quadrangle.

One rainy weekend morning, I went for a walk on campus. I parked just off Palm Drive, which connects the city of Palo Alto with the campus. The heart of the University is a huge, beautiful quadrangle, built in the late 19th century. Its old stones have mellowed with age. The University, now the nerve center of Silicon Valley, has expanded in all directions—but to me, the old part still represents Stanford University—at least emotionally. And not just to me, but also to the hordes of tourists who visit the campus and the Japanese brides in white with their future husbands taking photographs against the backdrop of the Memorial Church. In the rain, the old buildings seem a bit somber, though even more beautiful than in the sunshine. The rain runs off the shiny sides of the Rodin sculptures which stand in front of the oldest of the buildings. The palm trees, and the groves of eucalyptus, their bark peeling, their roots shallow in the soil—these still stand like sentinels, guarding the campus, making a kind of green belt or buffer between the quadrangle and the city of Palo Alto.

The psychology department is housed in one of the sections of the old quadrangle and it faces a grassy expanse called "the Oval." After hours, and on weekends, the psychology building would be locked up tight. I knew that, of course. You needed a key or a code or something to get in. Three people that I knew of could have easily gotten entrance. And the three of them *did* get in: Lissa, Mildred, and Philpott. Philpott admitted as much. They all had a key. But there could have been others. Members of the department. Griffin Peabody? Presumably he had a key, and he could have entered the building. And of course, Ramsey could have let somebody in. He could have gone down and opened the door. Perhaps there was a way of opening the outside door from his office. Maybe he was expecting a visitor.

Why did I think that was unlikely? Somehow I did. Why? I don't really know. But if we eliminate that idea, then there are three suspects who were absolutely there, and at least one more who *could* have been there. But why was Ramsey in his office at night in the first place? Catching up on his work? He was a prominent scholar, a productive scholar. All the obituaries talked about his passion for work. Maybe he had an urge to work on some project and needed some materials in his office. He had no home life, after all. He was estranged from his wife.

His children were grown and far away. Most likely he was at his computer—analyzing data from his latest study, or looking at material in his files—unaware that death was around the corner.

The rain stopped and, after a while, the sun peeped out from behind the clouds. I walked back to my car and went home.

22

Of course, as I knew, I shouldn't even be thinking about the case. But there I was. And the more I thought about it, the more I felt—the key is Lissa King. She's the only real connection we have between the murder of her sister and the murder of Ramsey Hardcastle. And she knows something, something she hasn't been telling me about. In addition, she's frightened. She knows something, and it's scaring her. I made up my mind to try to talk to her once more.

But while I was thinking about this, at my office on Monday, I had a call from Sylvan. "Let's have lunch, Frank," he said. "I have lots to talk to you about. And I've discovered a wonderful new restaurant in San Carlos, it's got a really hot chef, and it's fusion food, Asian-Italian. That's something new, Frank—Asian-French, that's old stuff—but Asian-Italian, that's worth considering."

I had my doubts about the cuisine, but Sylvan's enthusiasm carried the day. I found myself in a slick new restaurant in a booth with Sylvan, pondering a menu that had such wonders on it as "cappelletti with yellowtail sashimi," and "Florentine sushi with quail's egg." I'll spare you the details.

Sylvan loved the food. He smacked his lips and couldn't stop praising each item. "This is a real find, Frank," he said, "don't you agree?"

In fact, I didn't; but I nodded my head. No reason to disappoint Sylvan.

"You're going to be grateful to me, Frank, for two reasons. First, this restaurant. It's a gem."

"And the second one, Sylvan?"

He seemed so eager he could barely contain himself. "Frank, I've solved your case."

"*My* case, Sylvan? I don't have a case."

"Never mind. Whatever. Look: I figured out what happened. I set my razor-sharp legal mind to work and I got results! Let's start with this woman, Geena King, the body in that house, the mysterious body. Puzzles galore. How did somebody get into the house? And her car: gone one day and then the next day it appears, like out of nowhere, on the street. You told me about that, Frank."

"Yes, I did. So what? Look, Sylvan," I said, "Out with it. What's this brilliant idea you have?"

"I'll tell you. Remember: there's a key to the house. This kid, Teddy, he's got the key. Let's say, he comes in the morning, he opens the door, he waters the plants, he looks around, sees everything is in order, maybe he brings in the mail, whatever. So, the house, it's open when he's there. Maybe he doesn't even close the door behind him. Or he leaves it unlocked while he does his stuff, and only locks it again when he goes out.

"So what do you have? You have the house, it's open, and it's available. Now: our killer, let's say, is Ramsey Hardcastle. He's having an affair with Geena King, but it's a secret. Doesn't want anybody to know, especially her sister, because he and his secretary, they're lovers too. He's cheating on her, with her own sister. Now the sister's pregnant. Geena. She's expecting a baby. She meets Ramsey, maybe at his house, maybe someplace else. She comes in her car. Maybe he gets into the car, and they drive somewhere. They argue, they have a big fight, she demands that he get married or something and he loses his cool—and he strangles her. 'Oh, God, now what do I do?' he says to himself. He's got to get rid of the body. He wraps the body in something, and he puts it in his car. He's desperate. What's he going to do with it? He's driving around, and he sees Teddy opening the door to the Williams house. He sneaks the body inside. Then he hears Teddy—he's upstairs doing something—Ramsey panics, and stuffs the body in the chest. He hides, maybe, in the house. When Teddy leaves, he slips out himself. Nobody sees him.

"Teddy, he never noticed anything. Never saw Ramsey. Now Ramsey takes the car—he's got the keys, they were in Geena's purse—he drives Geena's car somewhere, maybe his house, puts it in his garage, and then he cleans it and cleans it to get rid of any evidence. Then, the next day, he parks it on the street. Hopes nobody will notice. But Teddy, he's a smart kid, so he's aware that the car wasn't there before and now, suddenly, there it is. So that's my solution to the puzzle. What do you think, Frank? Pretty clever, no? And it makes sense."

"I don't know, Sylvan. To me, it still sounds far-fetched. And you say Ramsey Hardcastle is the one who killed Geena King. But he's dead too. Who did *that*?"

"Well, who knows? Personally, I think it was his secretary, Lissa. When they find her sister, she puts two and two together. She confronts the guy, he admits it, all of it, the affair, the murder, and she kills him in revenge. She strangles him with her scarf. That makes sense too."

Makes sense? Not to me? But Sylvan was beaming; clearly the whole notion delighted him. "They've got killer desserts here," he said. "Let's try their tiramisu."

I opted for something else. I had to admit, the dessert was delicious, whatever I thought about the prior courses. We made small talk, exchanging gossip about some of our legal colleagues, and then we went our separate ways.

Sylvan's story did, I suppose, make a certain amount of sense. *Something* had happened for the body to end up inside Margot Williams' house. Maybe Teddy and his key was the crucial point after all, maybe I should concentrate on this particular point. But could Sylvan's story be right? Would Teddy really leave the door unlocked? How long was he in the house? I remembered that Teddy had, in fact, been at the house Sunday morning—he had said so. But when exactly was he there?

I made a mental note to ask Teddy if it was possible the door was left unlocked, and how long had he stayed in the house, and what time this happened. Teddy was in school, I supposed. I called Tina, and asked her to ask Teddy to get in touch with me. She said she would.

He called me back when he got home from school. I asked him to tell me about that Sunday morning. "It's important, Teddy."

"Wow, are you on to something? Anyway, I didn't stay long. I didn't do much, you know? I mean, they were due back, Margot and Jim. They said afternoon. So I didn't turn the lights on."

"What time were you there, Teddy?"

"I dunno. Late, maybe. I sleep late, Sunday. Mom says, if there was an earthquake, I'd sleep right through it. Sometimes I sleep 'til noon. But I think I was there earlier. Maybe it was eleven o'clock. Don't remember exactly."

"You wouldn't leave the door open, but while you were in the house, the door wasn't locked, was it?"

"Leave the door open? You think I'm crazy? And it was locked while I was there. I mean, I would go in the house, close the door behind me, you know. So you'd still need a key to get in."

"That's good, Teddy. That's helpful. Thank you."

"Hey, what's this about? You got a new idea? Something I could do to help you out?"

"No, Teddy no. Not now anyway."

So Sylvan's theory was full of holes. And yet ... something in the story stuck in my mind, wormed its way into my brain, and wouldn't let go. I couldn't put my finger on what it was. Not then, at any rate. Only later did the electric light bulb go off in my head.

23

Sylvan's lunch was an interlude, but a productive one. It wasn't really clear to me *how* productive it was. Not at the time.

I called Lissa's house. Nobody answered, and I left a message. I buried myself in work. I had a meeting with my friend, Zelda Valdez, the romance novelist. She had a new contract with a publisher and I had promised to look it over and tell her what I thought. The book was about a woman who was four hundred years old, but she still looked terrific, "because of this elixir, something they discovered, an ancient formula, Frank, and she never ages. But now she's in love, madly in love—his name is Felix, he's a brilliant and handsome young man, he's a medical resident, and he's doing research, and they have mad sex—but she hasn't told him her secret, he doesn't know she was born in Transylvania, and she has to take this stuff to keep on living and not getting old. Meanwhile, she's actually investigating the elixir that keeps her going, so there's this terrible conflict."

This was a change from Zelda's usual subject matter. She told me, "I've never done sci-fi before, but there's elements of science here, so I've been consulting a chemist to make the whole elixir thing seem kosher. I never had to do this sort of research before!"

I saw nothing wrong with the contract. The plot was another matter.

Zelda herself was unlucky in love. She had been married, actually, to Milo Feigenblatt, the avant-garde composer, and now she was "in the market for a guy, Frank, if you know anybody."

Zelda was a tough sell: I love her, but she's not what most men want. She's very tall, and not exactly beautiful, with her hooked nose, and sharp features. They make her look as if her natural mode of transportation was a broomstick.

I had a sudden thought: Milo! I asked Zelda whether she was on good terms with her ex-husband. She said, "Oh, we're good friends. He's on the loose again, poor man. His new woman, Zoe, she's pregnant, and that's good; but she walked out on him anyway, poor guy. Maybe it's not his baby. I see Milo every once in a while, he's good company. We just weren't right for each other."

They had always been an unlikely couple. Physically, anyway. She was tall, bony, and angular, with long, stringy black hair. He was short, pudgy, and bald. They were both—how should I put it?—eccentric. Milo had a thing for women whose names began with a Z. Zelda's last name, moreover, also ended with a Z; that was apparently what attracted him in the first place. Alas, this turned out not to be much of a basis for a lasting relationship, but I was glad to hear they were still good friends.

Milo was just about the only person I could think of who might possibly help me with the puzzle of Laszlo Szekely, the Hungarian violinist. Zelda gave me Milo's phone number, and I called him. He was, as usual, quite bubbly and friendly on the phone. Milo was a person of zest and energy, and extremely likeable.

I met Milo, I have to tell you, under odd circumstances, as I think I mentioned. It was when my dentist's receptionist, Maggie Swift, was murdered. Milo and I were both patients of that dentist.

It did not surprise when me when he said, "How're you doing, Frank? Any murders lately?"

"Actually, yes. I don't know why this sort of thing happens to me."

"Karma, Frank. Karma."

"Milo," I said, "I have to ask you a rather strange question. Do you know a violinist named Laszlo Szekely?"

"Laszlo? Sure I do," he said. "He's with the Farkas Quartet; I've had dealings with them. And with him, personally. I visited him in London, once—he had this flat in north London. I wanted him to do one of my pieces, a *Sonata for Violin and Chain Saw* and he was definitely interested, but it didn't work out. Not that time. But his quartet, they did one of my pieces, right here at Stanford. Did a good job, too. Why do you want to know?"

"It's a long story, Milo. Do you think there's a chance I could talk to him?"

"Well, I don't know where he is, at the moment. The Quartet travels a lot. They're successful, but they're not at the top of the heap, to be honest with you. They play in places like Boise, Idaho when they're in this country. But they did have this gig at Stanford, not that long ago, I could check on the date."

"Do that, Milo, and let me know, okay? But meanwhile, what can you tell me about this guy?"

"What do you mean, musically or what?"

"Well, actually, more about his personal life," I said. "Okay, here's the thing. A professor of psychology at Stanford, Ramsey Hardcastle, was murdered in his office. And he mentioned the name of Laszlo Szekely to somebody before he died, but we don't know why."

"Oh, I love it," Milo said. "I can see the whole scene. The professor is lying in a pool of blood, and as he's dying, he whispers the name of Laszlo Szekely."

"You've been reading too many of Zelda's books," I said. "It wasn't like that at all. Actually, what happened was this: before he was killed, a few days before, I think, he asked one of his assistants to check up on Szekely. Didn't give a reason."

I asked Milo if he knew about some possible connection between Szekely and Ramsey Hardcastle. He didn't. He had never heard of Hardcastle, in point of fact.

"But it's not like Laszlo and I are thick," he said. "I knew him professionally. I was in his house, only once. Boy, was he married to a bitch. An American woman, her name was Edith—

she was much younger than Laszlo. Not a happy marriage, and that's an understatement. Not that I'm one to talk, I'm a serial failure, I keep getting married, but it doesn't last. Still, I'm friendly with all my ex-wives and ex-girlfriends. And none of them were like Edith. I mean, we were trying to talk about music and I was showing him the score of my sonata, and she came in like gangbusters, yelling and screaming, God knows why. And poor Laszlo was so embarrassed. He told me, later, in his thick Hungarian accent, 'dat woman's gonna kill me someday,' and she threatened to smash his Stradivarius. They must be divorced by now, how could anybody stay married to a witch like that? But I don't actually know."

"Milo," I said, "could you do me an enormous favor? If you find out how to reach this guy, can you ask him, discreetly, how he was connected to Professor Ramsey Hardcastle of the Psychology Department of Stanford University?"

"Sure thing. I'll do my best."

* * *

It took a while, but in a few days, Milo called me back. "I talked to Laszlo. He was with the quartet and they were in Arkansas, 'playing to the yokels,' as he put it. It's too bad they don't get better bookings, in places like New York or Wigmore Hall in London. They don't dare do my music in Arkansas. In New York, there's an audience for my music, people who like new music, you know, they listen to the Kronos group, they're open-minded—but Arkansas is hopeless.

"Anyway, that's neither here nor there. I asked him if he knew Ramsey Hardcastle. He gave me a really funny answer. He said, 'thank God, no.' I said, 'did you ever meet him?' He said, 'I told you, no.' Then he said, 'Why would I want to?' Well, this was pretty peculiar, so I said, 'Could you explain yourself?' and he said, 'I could, Milo, but frankly, I won't.' And that was that."

On the surface, that was no help at all. If anything, it made the mystery of Laszlo Szekely deeper. He and Ramsey Hard-castle *were* connected, but how? And Ramsey had also mentioned another name to Griffin: Margot Williams. I should have asked Milo to ask Laszlo whether he knew Margot Williams. But if he had asked, I'm sure the answer would have been no. And both Margot and Jim claimed they had no idea who Laszlo Szekely was. It seemed to me extremely unlikely that they were connected, in any way, with a classical violinist of Hungarian descent.

And yet: there had to be something that tied Margot to this man. And that tied this man to Ramsey Hardcastle. And Ramsey Hardcastle to Geena King. But what could it be?

The only thing I could think of was Lissa King.

24

I had been trying to reach Lissa, without much luck. I suspected she was at home, but in no mood to answer the phone. I left messages. She ignored them at first, but then, rather suddenly, she called me back. It was midafternoon, and I was in my office.

I asked her how she was, and whether she had gone back to work. She sounded absolutely awful, and after a few sentences, she burst into tears. "Frank," she said, "I can't go on like this. Can you come to the house? I've got to talk to you."

I promised to come and as soon as I was able to, I got into my car and drove over to her house. I noticed the shades were still drawn.

I rang the bell. I heard sounds from inside, and the door was opened a crack. She called out, "Is that you, Frank?" I said yes, and she opened the door the rest of the way and let me in. I sat down in the living room. She asked me if I wanted anything, coffee or tea. I said no.

She looked bad. Her hair was uncombed, and there were those dark circles under her eyes. She said, "Frank, we have to talk."

I said, "Sure, Lissa. I'm here to listen."

"The police have come by again. They think I know something. It's that wretched scarf. They think I killed Professor Hardcastle. Frank, I couldn't kill anybody. But they ask so many questions. They think I'm lying. 'Why were you there? Isn't it odd you were in the man's office at night time?' They even asked me, point blank, 'Were you having an affair with this man?' I think that awful woman is talking to them."

"I'm really sorry," I said. "I know it's an ordeal. I'd love to help you, but, really, I don't see what I can do."

"I want you to hear the whole story. I haven't told this to anybody. The police think I am lying; and I am. I told them my boss was very demanding, and that I often went there at night. They said, 'Oh, is that so? Well, what did he want?' And I said he was working on a study, he had government funding, and there was a report due, and he wanted me to work on it, because of a deadline—and that was a lie, and I'm sure they're going to find out it's a lie. I don't know why I was so stupid, they can check, if there was really some kind of report due, and when they find out there's nothing to it, they'll be back and the torture will start all over again."

"Well, why don't you just tell them the truth?"

She was silent for a while. Then she said: "Because I can't. I just can't."

"I don't understand."

"After they ... found my sister's body, and I went back to work, he called me into his office. This was, oh, maybe a week after my sister died ... He said he had been getting threatening letters, and did I know anything about it? Unsigned letters. I don't read his mail ... I told him, 'No, I don't know anything about it. What did these letters say?' He said, 'I can't tell you. But it has something to do with your sister.' I said, 'My sister? What could they possibly have to do with my sister?' But he wouldn't tell me. He just said, 'Don't say anything about this, to anyone. Do you understand? To nobody.' He got very angry, and he was sort of, well, threatening. He was an awful person. Here I was, my sister was dead, I was all upset, and he was treating me that way."

"Go on."

"Then he said—and I don't know if there was any connection between what he said, and ... and anything—he asked me, 'Where are my old files?' I said, 'What old files?' and he said, 'Data, materials on experiments, hard copies, things from the days before they put everything on computers, where is all that?' and I said, 'Well, I think they're in storage, in the university warehouse, I really don't know.' And he said, 'You've got to find out. You've got to. Where's the storage? I've got a file number, would it be there, in that warehouse or whatever it is?' And I said, 'I guess so.' And he told me the file number, and he said, 'I want this. Write it down. And get it for me. But don't say a word to anybody.'"

"And did you?"

"I said I'd send for the stuff, and he said, 'No, I want you to go get this file. Tomorrow. Don't delay.' And he kept saying, 'Don't tell anybody. Not a word.'"

"So you went and got the file."

"Yes. I mean, I thought so. Fact is, I wrote the number down wrong—I was so nervous and upset—I reversed two numbers. Anyway, it was late in the day, and I had gone home, and he called me and said, 'Did you get the file?' And I said, 'Yes.' And he said, 'Bring it to me.' I said, 'Okay, first thing in the morning.' He said, 'No, now. Right now. Come to my office.'"

"And that's why you were there."

"Yes. I handed him the file, and he flew into a rage. He said, 'You fool, you idiot, this is the wrong file.' I never saw him so angry. He ... hit me, I was crying. He said, 'You damn fool, look what you've done! You get that file first thing tomorrow, or you're out of a job and I'll make sure you never work again. So just do it. Get it right this time. And don't tell anybody about any of this. Not anybody.' His face was all distorted, he was so angry.

"It was kind of chilly and I had come in a jacket and scarf. When I went into the office I took off the scarf and put it down ... But just then, I heard footsteps outside in the hall and Ramsey seemed to get even more agitated, he told me, 'Get out of here, now!' His office was connected to another room where I worked, so he opened the door and shoved me into that office, and whispered, 'Get the hell out of here, quick!' and I heard somebody knocking on his door as I let myself out using the back stairway. I never saw the person. I was very upset, I was crying. And then, to top it off, I saw that awful woman, Mildred, and Philpott Peabody, and ... she said awful things. I went home, I was in a terrible state. I slept in, I took a sleeping pill, but in the morning the police called me—they woke me up, and they told me ... somebody had killed him—and they seemed to know already that it was my scarf, maybe somebody at the office recognized it, and this whole ordeal got worse and worse."

"And you have no idea who that was, that other person, the one who came in? Was the professor expecting him? Or her?"

"Oh, Frank, I have no idea. I was just upset and I got out of there, I ran away."

"The building was locked, Lissa. How did that person get in?"

"Maybe he had a key. The faculty, they all have keys. Mildred has a key. Or maybe a cleaning lady let somebody in. I just don't know."

"Could you talk to them, the cleaning staff?"

"Oh, Frank, no—I don't know who they are and most of them don't speak English. And ... I just can't."

"Did you tell this to the police? This story?"

"No, I didn't. At first, I was just so upset, I mean, a second murder, and I was involved—and they got it into their heads that I was connected, well, I *was* connected—my sister, my boss, and I didn't want to tell them about the file. Listen, Frank, here's what I think was going on. He needed that file, for somebody, somebody who was coming to see him, and when this person got there, it was the wrong file, and ... that's why somebody killed him. And I thought, what if Professor Hardcastle said, to this person, 'My secretary, she got the wrong file,' I thought, I'll be next on his list, whoever he is."

"So you never got the file. The right file."

"Oh, no; I mean, he was dead, and so what was the point? So I never did. But listen, Frank, a while after that, couple of days I think, I got a phone call, somebody whispering in a funny voice, and I hung up, and I thought, oh God, maybe somebody is after me, and it freaked me out totally. And I think I know who it is."

"Who, Lissa?"

"I think it might be that Hungarian person. Griffin told me about him. The one Professor Hardcastle was asking all kind of questions about. I think this must be the man who was threatening him. Writing letters. I mean, he might be somebody from organized crime. Why was Professor Hardcastle interested in this Hungarian? I can't remember his name, you asked me about him, and I said I didn't know him—and I don't, I have no idea who he is. Maybe he killed my sister, or maybe Professor Hardcastle killed my sister, God knows why, I mean, he asked Griffin to check out Margot Williams, too, there's something really creepy going on, and, Frank, I'm just plain scared. Can you help me?"

"I'll try, Lissa; but really, I'm just a lawyer. You need to go to the police ..." but she shook her head and said no, no, she couldn't.

I didn't know what I could do for her. But I had a sudden inspiration. "Lissa," I said, "you have to go get that file. The file the Professor wanted. We have to see what's in that file."

"Oh, Frank, must I?"

"I think you must. I really do, Lissa. There might be something in that file. I want you to get it. We'll read it, and if it has some, well, relevance to all of this, we'll turn it over to the police. You'll tell them the whole story."

She was clearly reluctant, but I insisted. I said it might be a way for her to get clear of this mess she was in. Maybe that file was the key to the mystery. Maybe it would tell us why somebody felt they had to kill Ramsey Hardcastle. At last she agreed.

As it turned out, my instincts were correct.

25

I went home, had a good dinner, watched a program on television, and went to bed. I slept soundly, for a change. The alarm clock woke me in the morning.

Lissa called me in the late morning. She thanked me for coming over, and said she was "feeling much better. You're going to help me, I know it."

"Well, I hope so," I said. "Did you get the file? Did you read it?"

"I have it," she said. "I'm not sure what it means. I want you to read it, Frank. Can you come over? Tonight, I mean. I'm at work now."

I felt glad that Lissa had gone to work instead of brooding in her place with the shades drawn. I told Celia I had to visit someone after dinner and I managed to evade the questioning. I guess she thought it was a client. Is it a lie if you don't correct a misperception? I hope not.

I drove over to Lissa's. She let me in, and I noticed that the shades were no longer drawn. That was a good sign. She handed me the file, and I took it to a table in the next room to read it carefully.

It was a description of some of Ramsey Hardcastle's earlier work. It was not a file that contained actual data, but it was a sort of notebook in which he recorded his thoughts during some of his experiments. In the document, which was marked "confidential," I saw a familiar name. There was another name that I was not quite so familiar with, but recognized—and I knew its significance too.

When I saw those names, the electric light bulb went off in my brain. There was a lot I didn't understand, not immediately. But I thought I knew who had killed Ramsey Hardcastle. And, presumably, the same person had killed Geena King. I didn't quite understand the motives, not yet. I sat there, though, pondering. I started thinking about the puzzle that started this whole business off: how had the body ended up in Margot's house, who put it there, and why? I still didn't know the why, but the more I thought about it, the more I felt sure I understood the how. And that was the crucial point.

"Lissa," I said, "this is really important. It has to go to the police."

She kept shaking her head no. She wanted nothing to do with the police.

"Okay," I said, "let me take care of it." I took the file home with me. I suppose that was vaguely illegal, but I didn't care.

I have to say, I felt the same way Lissa did. I want to have nothing to do with the police, if at all possible. I don't know any police officers, I mean, not personally. My only contact is with the traffic police, and my blood turns to ice when I'm driving and I see a police car, behind me, next to me, in front of me, or anywhere. I always imagine they'll arrest me for *something*. Celia tells me, over and over again, what a terrible driver I am. I'm sure she's right. But I'm not a drunk driver, I don't play chicken, I usually follow the rules. Well, most of them. Still, the police always scare me.

So, no, I didn't go to the police. I called up my friend Nolan Thom, the criminal lawyer—he has all sorts of contacts, he's smart, he's worldly, and he always knows what to do—I told him I needed to see him. As soon as possible, I said. We fixed a time.

Then, when we got together, I told him as much as I knew; he was generally familiar with the issue—with the two murders. I told him I assumed the police had gotten nowhere, and he said he thought that was correct. Then I showed him the file. At first, he didn't see what I was driving at, but I spelled it out for him. "I could be wrong," I said, "but I don't think so." We talked for a while. Then he said, "Okay, I get the point. Leave it to me."

He was as good as his word. I'm not sure what he did, or who he talked to, but he got results. Within a few days, the police made an arrest. I read about it in the local newspaper. "Double Murder Solved," was the headline. I was glad it was over, but in all honesty, I couldn't be happy about the result. It was a personal tragedy for the people involved. But murder is murder, and there was no real alternative.

26

Sometimes, the solution to a puzzle is so obvious that nobody sees it. I mean, if something is obvious, looks obvious, and acts obvious, it probably *is* obvious. And when you thought about it, there was something about the death of Geena King that was completely obvious. Or should have been. Only it wasn't. Not to me, or to anybody else. But perhaps I'm not being fair. There was, after all, a darn good reason why we couldn't see the obvious.

The newspapers made much more of a fuss about Ramsey Hardcastle than they did over Geena King. Ramsey was, after all, a famous man. A leading psychologist, a giant in his field, a man with an entry in Wikipedia and several honorary degrees. I imagine the police, too, spent more time and energy trying to solve that case. But what was the motive for killing Ramsey Hardcastle? That was a puzzle. True, nobody liked him. People in his department had a grudge against him. Mildred hated him. He had ruined Philpott's career. But, in the end, those emotions were not the reason why Ramsey Hardcastle got himself killed.

The true reason was highly unusual. People murder for love, for hate, for money, for revenge. None of these explained the death of Ramsey Hardcastle. He was murdered because of his research.

The death of Geena King unlocked the mystery. The first big question was this: How did the body get in Margot's house? And why would anybody put it there? There were several theories, none of them particularly convincing. Some of them turned on Teddy Gilchrist's key. Did somebody get hold of that key? He wore it around his neck, he slept with it—it almost never left his body. Still, getting the key was not, after all, impossible. He was a deep sleeper. He took showers— sometimes. His mother could have gotten the key, somehow, and made a copy. She could have given that copy to somebody. To Griffin, maybe. But why would she do that? And why would Griffin, or whoever, use the key to deposit a dead body in the house where Margot and Jim Williams lived? Why would that person drag a dead body there, presumably in broad daylight, open the door, and stuff Geena King into a chest at the foot of the stairs? Why on earth?

Did that person think nobody would bother looking for the body in that house? But, to put it crudely, if you hide a dead body in a house, even if nobody notices it, after a few days go by, a dead body becomes painfully obvious.

No, this didn't make sense. Nor did Sylvan's theory make sense. There was something we were all missing. But Sylvan's crazy idea did start me thinking. The body in the house. How on earth did it get there?

The simplest, most obvious explanation had nothing to do with Teddy and his key. If you knew some people had gone on a trip, and now they've come back from their trip, and you asked, how did this suitcase get in the house? You would say, that's a silly question: they brought it in with them. Of course. Here is the home of Margot and Jim Williams. If you ask, who besides Teddy had a key to the house, the answer is obvious. They did. Margot Williams had a key. Jim Williams had a key. So, if the question is: how did the body get in the house? The simplest answer would be: Margot and Jim (or just one of them) had brought it into the house.

Yet that seemed both senseless and impossible. Senseless, because Margot said, and I believed her, that she had never met this woman and had no idea who she was. Impossible, because Margot and Jim were in Carmel when the woman died, and Carmel was far away, maybe a hundred miles or so. A good two-hour drive, under the best of conditions.

If I eliminated Margot—for the sake of argument—then who was left? Her husband Jim. And, when I looked at the file, when I read the document, his name jumped out at me: James Williams. I also saw another name: Edith Davis. I saw the context. All this started me thinking. And I came to a firm conclusion: Jim Williams had murdered Geena King.

I mean, some people have this crazy idea that I'm some sort of great detective. A latter day Sherlock Holmes, or Hercule Poirot, or maybe even Sam Spade. I'm nothing of the sort. But I'm not a complete idiot, either, and once I saw a few essential facts, I could put two and two together. Jim Williams. It had to be him. First, he was the one who killed Geena King. And later, he must have killed Dr. Ramsey Hardcastle too. Of course, there was no proof—just the fact that his name was in that file. I still had no idea how and why this had been done.

But I had learned one vital fact. There *was* a connection between Jim Williams and Ramsey Hardcastle. Jim Williams, as a boy, had been "Little Willie," the subject of Ramsey's awful experiments inducing anger and frustration in children. There were two vivid experiments; case studies that he wrote up using (of course) assumed names. One of these wretched kids, victims of Hardcastle's rather sadistic research, was Jim Williams, his name disguised as "little Willie." There was also "Little Anna." For the moment, I ignored her. I focused on "Little Willie." It tied Jim Williams to Hardcastle, the professor who had tampered with his brain when he was a kid. And he was tied to the other victim too: she was found dead in his house.

At the very least, this made him a suspect. I felt sure he was more than a suspect; I felt he must be the killer. I passed this on to Nolan—everything I knew and suspected—actually, it wasn't that much, as yet; and Nolan went to the police. He told them that he had found this connection between Jim Williams and both of the victims and that this was something that was, at least, worth looking into.

And that made all the difference. Once they had a name, and a suspicion, the rest turned out to be surprisingly easy. They knew what to look for and where to look. Pretty soon it was all over. In a couple of days, they arrested Jim, and charged him with both murders. And at that point, the whole story came out. Jim Williams essentially gave up. He broke down and cried; he admitted everything. He said he hated himself, he said he hated what he had done, what he had become—it was all the professor's fault—he was a victim himself. But he signed a full confession. The gist of it was reported in the newspapers. They didn't get everything right, they never do, but the core element was there. Nolan told me the rest.

The story began in Los Angeles. In Los Angeles, Jim Williams somehow met Geena King. They became seriously involved. Apparently, though, it was more serious for her than for him. A bit later, he met Margot at an office party; they talked, they took a liking to each other, they had coffee together, they started dating. He said nothing about his involvement with Geena King. Indeed, as he got serious about Margot, he told Geena he was through. He tried to break off relations with her.

But she refused to accept this. She wanted him back. She demanded it. She was a strong, obstinate woman. Still, Jim had more or less committed himself to Margot. Indeed, Margot was pregnant. She still knew nothing about Geena. Jim kept that a secret. And to Geena, he insisted that their affair was over, dead, it was history—he was going to marry Margot, and, in fact, they did get married. They had a small, quiet wedding. He felt ready to move on. Start a new life.

Margot miscarried; maybe at that point Jim regretted marrying her. But he said nothing. He and Margot moved to the Bay Area. They found jobs, a house—their lives seemed to run more smoothly. He put Geena out of his mind. But she was infatuated and she couldn't get over him. She left her home in Los Angeles, moving in with her sister not far from the house where Margot lived with Jim. She got in touch with Jim, secretly of course. She insisted on seeing him. She sent him messages, letters, she phoned him at work.

He should have said no, should have told Margot the truth, but he was weak and foolish. He began meeting Geena at odd times and places and they soon had a sexual relationship. Jim claimed he tried to break it off, but Geena refused to hear of it.

She was also pregnant by now. She threatened to tell Margot. When he went to Carmel, with Margot, Geena followed him there. She found out where he was staying. She somehow got in touch with him, and insisted on a meeting.

On Sunday, he got up early in the morning, drove off and met her at a lonely stretch of the beach, by arrangement. Margot was asleep. Geena gave him an ultimatum: he must leave Margot, get a divorce, and marry her. He refused. He said they were finished and he told her to get an abortion—he told her he would never see her again, and that was that. They had a terrible quarrel, shouting and screaming at each other on the beach. Then, as he put it, he lost control of himself, his anger overwhelmed him: "Everything went blank, I don't know what came over me," and (this was his account), he strangled her with his mind in a kind of fog, almost without knowing what he was doing. "When I came to my senses, she was dead." At any rate, that's what he said. Whether it was exaggerated, or an actual lie, I have no way of knowing.

But there he was. Nobody had seen him. Panic set in. He had no idea what to do. He stuffed her body in the trunk of his car. He had no real plan, only a wild idea of somehow getting rid of the body. He drove back to their hotel. By this time, Margot was up. He was in terrible trouble, and he knew it. It was time to go home. They checked out, and started driving back—he was at the wheel. He managed to avoid opening the trunk; they didn't have much luggage, and he put everything in the back seat of the car. He was, of course, in a desperate state, but he managed to keep control of his nerves. He must have suffered terribly on the trip. There were some awful moments— like when they stopped, and Margot almost bought an antique chair; it would have had to go in the trunk. But he managed to talk her out of the idea; they didn't buy the chair, and the crisis passed.

They got home after dark. He waited until Margot went upstairs, then, quickly, he opened the trunk and shoved the body into the cedar chest. He intended to get rid of it somehow at night, bury it somewhere, or throw it in the bay. He wasn't thinking straight. He felt if he could do that, he would be in the clear. Maybe the body would never be found. How was he to know that Margot had stashed a gift for him in that chest, under the linens, and that she would open it up and find the body? His horror and dismay were real enough; Margot herself was terrifically upset, and his reaction seemed only natural to her.

He had taken Geena's purse, and her car keys. He threw the purse into a dumpster and pocketed the keys. On Monday, he took off from work—he flew to Monterey, took a cab to Carmel, with the keys, and drove her car back to the Bay Area. He parked the car on the street, hoping nobody would notice that it hadn't been there before. Hoping, too, that when Geena's body was finally identified, that they would assume she had never left the area. Of course, he was running a terrible risk, but nobody—he hoped—would bother to check on his comings and goings. There was no obvious connection with Geena King. And it seemed impossible to link him with the case. Nobody would suspect that she had died in Carmel, that she had been driven to the Bay Area in the trunk of his car.

Of course, once the police were tipped off—once they were told he was a suspect, once he was on their radar screen—the rest was simple. The plane trip to Monterey, and all of the rest of his actions, were easy to track. There were no traces of blood or the like in Geena's car, which they had impounded— naturally, because the body had never been in it. In his car, on the other hand, they found evidence. He had, of course, cleaned out the trunk as best he could, but there was enough left to incriminate him—despite his best efforts—once they realized it was the right place to look.

And Ramsey Hardcastle? Jim had never forgotten that man. As he brooded, half-wild with fear and anguish, he began to blame Hardcastle for the tragedy that had overtaken him. He was, after all, "Little Willie." The professor had played mind games with him, had destroyed his personality (he felt), and had given him an uncontrollable temper. True, he was usually able to rein in that temper, but once in a while it flared up and, when it did, he blamed it all on Ramsey Hardcastle. It was

Hardcastle who had made a murderer out of him. All of his misery was really Hardcastle's fault.

And perhaps only Ramsey Hardcastle could help him. He felt sure he would be caught, eventually. He would be accused of murder. Hardcastle, though, could say it was not Jim's fault. He could reveal that Jim Williams was "Little Willie," and that the real Jim Williams was not a murderer—Hardcastle had destroyed his personality—Williams had not really killed Geena King. The real killer was "Little Willie," now grown-up, but damaged beyond repair. And in a way, Professor Hardcastle was the guilty party, at least in Jim's mind. In a sense, he was the one who had strangled Geena King.

Jim started sending letters to the professor; I think Hardcastle considered this behavior quite threatening. I'm not sure exactly what Jim told him. Hardcastle destroyed the letters, and nobody else saw them. But they gave Hardcastle something to think about. He was interested, both personally and academically. Maybe he had wondered, for some time, what had become of these two famous subjects. Now he had some information: Jim was Little Willie, and the results had been disastrous. He wondered what had become of his other famous subject, Little Anna. He found out that she was married to a Hungarian violinist, Laszlo Szekely. What was she like? He gave Griffin the names of the two spouses. He was too cautious to mention Jim Williams and Edith Szekely. What he wanted to know was, how had they turned out? He felt this was something their spouses could tell better than anybody else. Had the experiments done something to Jim and to Edith? Had it done, or seemed to do, permanent damage?

Ironically, Jim Williams had seemed, on the surface, quite normal: His life with Margot was smooth and free from violence. Perhaps the violence was all bottled up, and only came out in frantic outbursts, and only rarely—like when Geena threatened to destroy the basis of his life. Edith, on the other hand, was overtly disturbed. She made life a living hell for her Hungarian husband. I think Laszlo knew, or came to know, her history, which would explain his odd remarks to Milo Feigenblatt, his remarks about Ramsey Hardcastle.

In any event, there was a fateful meeting in Ramsey Hardcastle's office. I think Jim had called him and demanded to see him. Ramsey let him in—or the cleaning people let him in—anyway, he confronted Ramsey in his office. But Ramsey flatly refused to do anything for Jim—he insisted his experiment had been "harmless," claimed that it was not traumatic at all; that there was no reason to believe it had lasting effects. I wonder if he actually believed that. We'll never know. There was one piece of evidence that he felt a certain amount of guilt: his codicil, making provision for Geena's sister. But according to Jim, when the two of them talked, Hardcastle insisted that whatever happened had been entirely Jim's fault, and not his. He said (again, according to Jim), that he was going to turn Jim over to the police. Then came a terrible quarrel, and another rage, and a total blackout; and when Jim came to his senses, Ramsey Hardcastle was dead. Jim had strangled him with Lissa's scarf.

I don't know if I believe all of this story. The blackout part, for example, seems awfully convenient. Jim hired a very good lawyer—a criminal lawyer named Logan Faircloth, a good friend of Sylvan's. Sylvan told me, over lunch, that Jim and Logan had a difficult choice to make: go to trial, and try to persuade the jury that Jim was not fully responsible—that he had blacked out and had no memory of actually killing these people—and that the real villain was Ramsey Hardcastle and his diabolical experiments, which had ruined Jim for life. Maybe Edith Szekely could be brought in or Laszlo. The hope was that the jury would vote to acquit, or at least find him guilty of some lesser crime. But that tactic was risky; it would be a very hard sell. In the end, Jim took a deal which the prosecution offered: he pleaded guilty to second-degree murder. His new home is San Quentin.

* * *

You have to feel sorry for Margot. All this, as you can imagine, came as a terrible shock to her. She was pregnant, and alone. Her husband had cheated on her, and—worse than that—he was a killer. She filed for divorce. After the baby was born, she sold the house and moved away; I think she went to Cincinnati, where she had some family connections. I lost all contact with her. Rumor was, she got an amazing price for the house. Houses in the Bay Area sell as if they were plated with solid gold leaf. You have to wonder who on earth can afford them, but obviously, some people can. Young billionaires from the hi-tech world.

I did wonder, though, whether she got full market value for the house. Some people might feel queasy about a home which once held a dead body hidden in a chest, near the stairs. A house whose co-owner was a double murderer, now sitting in San Quentin. But it takes all kinds. Some people might find that little fact a plus, something that gives them a heady, almost intoxicating feeling. Something they can talk to their friends about. Houses in that neighborhood all look alike; they're boringly the same. But only the Williams house is haunted by its past.

I had very little contact after that, either with Tina Gilchrist, or with Teddy. I hope Tina found somebody nice through the internet, and I hope Teddy gets into a good college. He's got the brains and the grades. I started having regular lunches with Sylvan. He has a nose for unusual restaurants and I don't mind capitalizing on his skills. Sylvan made a fat fee from the estate of Ramsey Hardcastle. It was, in a way, hardly worth it. "I earned it ten times over," he told me. That was because of Mildred Hardcastle. She sued the estate, sued him, sued the University, sued everybody under the sun.

As for me, I went back to my humdrum existence. I did go, I have to say, to a chamber music concert given by the Farkas Quartet in San Jose. I was curious to take a look at Laszlo Szekely. He had not the slightest resemblance to Bela Lugosi. He looked, in fact, quite ordinary: middle aged, with thinning hair, and a roman nose, but otherwise, nothing special. I'm not sure I'm a judge of chamber music. The first item on the program was a quartet by Franz Josef Haydn. That seemed quite nice. But afterwards came something totally incompre-hensible, by one of Milo Feigenblatt's students. I remember very little about it, except that it was screechingly ugly, and the poor musicians had to talk as well as play—reciting some poem out loud that was as dismal as the music. I must say, Laszlo looked quite unhappy, but maybe this was just my imagination.

I left at the intermission.

.

About the author

LAWRENCE FRIEDMAN is a professor of law at Stanford University. He teaches courses in American legal history and law and society. He is the author of *A History of American Law, Crime and Punishment in American History, The Human Rights Culture,* and *Total Justice,* among other works. Professor Friedman has also published *The Big Trial: Law as Public Spectacle* and, most recently, *Impact: How Law Affects Behavior.* His book *Dead Hands: A Social History of Wills, Trusts, and Inheritances* deals with a subject that is the backbone of Frank May's (fictional) practice.

Visit us at *www.qpbooks.com.*

www.ingramcontent.com/pod-product-compliance
Lightning Source LLC
Chambersburg PA
CBHW051121260626
47170CB00005B/1612